JESSICA WATKINS PRESENTS

A Rapper's DELIGHT

CHARAE LEWIS

A
Rapper's
DELIGHT

PROLOGUE

"So, can you tell me how you ended up at the hotel?" Detective Cowan asked Fabian.

Fabian released a sigh. "I told you, she had a piece of my jewelry and my credit card, so I went to go get it after my show," he said for the fourth time.

"Okay, so you went to get it and what happened from there?"

"When I got there, we started to argue. She told me if I didn't want to be with her, she would kill herself and went on the balcony. I didn't believe her, so I went to leave. Then I heard the railing break on the balcony. I ran to the balcony and saw that she.... had jumped." It pained Fabian to repeat that part of the story.

"So why was the hotel room in shambles?" the detective asked with a raised brow.

Fabian huffed in frustration. "Because I was trying to look for my stuff. She wouldn't give it to me. That's how she operated. She played a lot of fucking games."

"Explain to me why there was a bruise on the victim's right cheek?" the detective asked.

Fuck! Fabian thought to himself. He had forgotten all about the slap that he had delivered to her. *Damn, should I tell the truth or what? This mothafucka looking at me like I killed her ass.*

"I don't know," Fabian lied.

"I think you do know. You were the last person to see her before her death. A lot of things are not adding up to me."

Fabian gave him a screw face. "What the hell you tryin' to say? You think I had something to do with her death?" Fabian asked incredulously.

The detective stood and began to pace around the room slowly. "You go see her to get a so-called necklace and credit card, which wasn't found in the room by the way. Then she has a bruise on her cheek, you don't know how it got there, and now you're saying she jumped to her death. This sounds like bullshit," Detective Cowan barked.

"I didn't do shit to her! I'm telling you the truth! What the fuck I gotta lie for?" Fabian yelled.

"What do you have to lie for?" the detective mocked. "You're one of the top selling rappers in the industry. You have several endorsement deals. Your album has sold over a million records and your career has skyrocketed to the top. So, yeah, you have a lot to lose, but truth be told, you're going to jail for murder, Mr. Fabian Bryant."

CHAPTER 1

♫ *Bitch we gutta, bitch we gutta*

M,I,L to the W

Not my brother or my mother

Hell nah, I don't trust ya

Hell nah, I don't trust ya ♫

Fabian sat in the studio listening to the track he had just recorded. He had been recording so much lately that it was as if he lived in the booth. Being an independent rap artist was never easy, but in the end, it was always rewarding. Fabian's last mixtape had exceeded his expectations and was certified platinum. Now he was being featured on the hottest rapper's songs as well as singers.

"Aye, this gon' be my last track for the night," Fabian declared.

Fabian was dead tired and was in need of some sleep. He had been on the go for the last forty-eight hours; from photo shoots to radio interviews, it was a never-ending ride. After laying down his last song, Fabian grabbed his keys, then shot out the door. While walking to his car, he inhaled the night air, appreciating the clear sky; he had always been a night owl. He hopped in his BMW 750i and sped off. Most times when he was coming from the studio, he chose to ride in silence while he became lost in his thoughts. So many events had been going on in his life that he never got a chance to think, let alone be by himself.

Since forever, he wanted to be a rapper. Seeing rap legends like Notorious B.I.G., Rakim and Tupac dominate the rap game inspired Fabian to go after his dreams. He started recording in his cousin's studio with the bare minimum. Since Fabian's brother, Braylon, had experience producing music for local artists in Milwaukee, he took on the role as music producer. Two successful mixtapes later and tons of radio play, Fabian was ready to take his place as top rapper in the game.

Walking into his ten thousand square foot Georgia home, he dropped his keys on the table in the foyer. Fabian was proud of his four bedroom, five-bathroom home. It was his dream home. He'd hired an interior decorator to enhance his space, and he couldn't have been happier. His house consisted of a media room, library, swimming pool and studio, of course.

He grabbed an orange juice out of the fridge, then headed upstairs to his lavish bedroom, where his girlfriend, Fancy, of two years was sitting in the middle of his king-sized bed. As soon as she saw Fabian, she instantly hopped up and proceeded to go in on him.

"Where have you been? It's been two days since I've seen you, and you can't call me?" she shot.

"Aye, sit your ass down. I don't feel like hearing all that shit tonight," Fabian fussed.

"Don't give me that, Fabe. I wanna know why I haven't received a call from you all day," she demanded.

Fabian huffed. "After my flight landed, I went straight to the studio. You know I don't answer my phone once I'm in the studio. Why you trippin' like you don't know the rules?" he said, speaking with a mean scowl.

Fancy softened her face. "I'm sorry, babe. It's just that I miss you," she purred while caressing the side of his face.

Fancy kissed him deeply on the lips and smiled. She watched intently as Fabian got undressed. Standing at 6'1", Fabian was the definition of a heartthrob with pecan colored skin and almond shaped shimmering eyes. He had a slender nose with soft succulent lips. With his low, curly cut and freshly trimmed beard, he always turned heads. Fancy still couldn't get over how lucky she was to be Fabian's leading lady. They had met at an industry party two years prior and the rest was history.

"You tired, baby?" Fancy asked, as he got under the covers.

"That ain't even the word. I'm exhausted," Fabian answered as he was dozing off.

"Baby, I was thinking; instead of a Range Rover, I would rather get the BMW 745i. I know the cost is a little steep, but I really want this… Fabe are you listening?" Fancy nudged him only to be ignored. She looked over at his face as the loud snore filled the room.

This nigga, she thought.

CHAPTER 2

"Kylie, did you get the samples that Jeremy Scott sent us?" Kylie's assistant and cousin, Kellan, asked.

"I did, but I haven't looked at them yet," Kylie said typing up an email on her Macbook.

Kellan popped her lips. "Well, you better look through them. You know you have to style Nicki Minaj for the VMA awards."

Kylie sucked her teeth. "Girl, I know, let me finish this email, and then I will look. Is that okay with you?" she snapped.

"Lose the attitude before Hillside starts to show," Kellan joked, referencing to a housing project in Milwaukee.

"Girl, bye. You'll still get your ass whooped."

Kylie was the top stylist in the entertainment business. She owned a styling company, in which she hired entry level stylists and would book clients for them. So far, her company was doing great and had brought in revenue of 1.4 million dollars. Kylie had worked with people such as Jennifer Aniston, Rihanna and even Patti Labelle. Her work was never done when celebrities requested that she style them for events. On top of that, Kylie was launching her jewelry line, *Eilyk,* which was her name spelled backward.

With her extremely busy workflow, Kylie never got any time for herself. Her world consisted of making others look beautiful.

After sending her fourteenth email for the day, Kylie closed her eyes and envisioned herself lying in Turks and Caicos with no cell phone and no laptop. Kylie was in desperate need of a vacation and a male companion.

All of her life, Kylie had been a hopeless romantic. Every man she had ever had a relationship with either cheated or gave her a lame excuse not to be with her. For years, Kylie struggled with thoughts of not being good enough.One failed relationship after another discouraged Kylie, so after her last relationship, she vowed to never love again.

"Look, Ky," Kellan said, interrupting her thoughts. "Jeremy sent some bomb ass pieces," she gloated.

Kylie walked over and went through the racks of clothing. As usual, he had shown out when designing his pieces.

"Yeah, I could see Nicki rocking this," Kylie said more to herself.

Kellan smacked her lips. "Fuck Nicki. I could see *me* rocking this," she joked.

Kylie giggled. "You're a mess. Here; pack up these clothes for me. I gotta make a quick run."

Kylie grabbed her clutch and shot out of the door. She hopped in her truck and cruised the streets of Milwaukee. She wanted to catch the local thrift store before it closed. Most people thought Kylie spent hundreds on her wardrobe, when in reality half of her clothes came from the thrift store. Kylie truly believed that the person made the clothes, not the other way around. And she liked some of the retro pieces that were available for so cheap. They put her in the mind of the old slow jams that she listened to. She loved to listen to old vinyl records by the late Billie Holliday and Etta James. Her mother always told her that she was an old soul. She didn't care for the music of her generation. Billie Holiday and Etta James sung about real love, the type of love that Kylie was having so much difficulty obtaining.

While sitting at a stop light, Kylie looked at herself in the rearview mirror. *What is wrong with me? Why can't I have a man that loves me?* she asked herself.

It wasn't like Kylie was ugly. In fact, she looked better than most of the celebrities she styled. Kylie had umber colored skin with slanted dark eyes and rosy cheeks. Her lips put Erykah Badu's lips to shame and her jet black, silky hair flowed to her shoulders. She had a body that most people considered thick, with her D cup breasts, and perfectly shaped bottom. She didn't have the flattest stomach, but it wasn't overlapping. Even with the beauty she possessed, Kylie feared being alone for the rest of her life. One thing was for certain, Kylie refused to settle for just being a girlfriend; she wanted that lifetime commitment.

****

Fabian was doing heavy promotion for his upcoming album, and had just finished a radio interview. His single had reached number two on the billboard charts, and he had been asked to be on the cover of Rolling Stone magazine. He was ecstatic, to say the least, because he was making moves without a deal. Most independent artists didn't get the recognition they deserved because of lack of money for promotion and distribution. Fabian didn't have that problem since he already had money.

Fabian used to be a heavy hitter in the dope game but unlike other d-boys, he knew hustling wasn't the end for him. He first started hustling because his mom was struggling with bills. He hated seeing his mother in that predicament so he started selling coke. Soon after, he graduated to selling heroin and was getting money out of the ass. He knew if he wanted to start a label of his own, he would need plenty of money. So, he stacked his bread, only spending if he needed to, and started his rap career. By far, that had been the best life decision he had made.

"What's the schedule for tomorrow?" Fabian asked his brother, Braylon, who was his manager.

"We gotta fly to New York to shoot this cover and hit up some more radio stations."

Fabian nodded his head. "Aight. Well, take me to my car. I'ma go see Kenyon," he said, referring to his son.

"Aight, bro. Tell my nephew I ain't forgot about him. I'm gon' still get him that 2K."

Fabian twisted his face. "Man, please. I already took care of that. His daddy always comes through," he joked.

"Man, whatever. Don't forget our flight leaves early in the morning, fam."

"Aight. I'm out."

Fabian hopped out and made his way to see his son. It had been more than a week since he'd last seen Kenyon, and Fabian was missing him dearly. The only con of being a successful rap artist was being away from his son. Fabian called him often, but it wasn't the same as spending time with him.

When he arrived at the house, Fabian jumped out, then rang the doorbell. After a minute, Ava, Kenyon's mother, answered the door.

"Hey, what brings you by?" Ava asked, stepping to the side to let him in.

"Just came to see my little man. Where is he?"

"He's in the basement playing his game."

Fabian quietly walked down the stairs and saw Kenyon yelling at the TV. Kenyon looked exactly like Fabian but with a brighter complexion. He was a smart six-year-old with a hilarious personality.

"Why are you talking to yourself?" Fabian joked, startling Kenyon.

"Dad!" Kenyon yelled, running towards him.

Fabian scooped him up, then gave him a bear hug. "What's up, man? Daddy missed you."

"I missed you too, dad. I wish you weren't gone so much," he said sadly.

Fabian sat him down, then kneeled in front of him. "Daddy gotta work so you can have the best of everything. When school lets out, I promise you can stay with me for the whole summer, aight?"

"Cool. Does Fancy have to come with us?" Kenyon asked.

"Why you ask me that?" Fabian quizzed.

Kenyon shrugged. "'Cause I like when it's just me, you and uncle Braylon," he said sweetly.

"We'll cross that bridge when we get to it, okay? Now come and get this ass whooping in this 2K."

"Dad, you can't hold me," Kenyon teased.

"Well, show me then," Fabian challenged.

They played a total of four games before Kenyon had to go to bed. Fabian made sure he showered before he tucked him in. It was times like this that Fabian cherished. Being a father was very serious to him, and he wanted to do his best in that role.

"Aight, man, I love you. I'll call you tomorrow, okay?" Fabian assured, pulling the covers up to Kenyon's neck.

"Okay. I love you too, dad."

Fabian closed Kenyon's door, then headed towards the kitchen where Ava was seated. She sat comfortably eating a slice of cheesecake. Sometimes Fabian would wonder what they would've been if Ava hadn't revealed to him that she was a lesbian. At first, he was shocked, but there were plenty of signs that told him she really was into women.

"What's up with you? You need some money?" he asked.

Ava shook her head. "Actually, I'm good. I still have money left over from the last time. Thanks."

"Aight. Let me know if you need more. I'm out," he announced.

"Okay. Turn the lock for me."

Fabian hurried and hopped in his ride. He wanted to get a full night's rest, since the following day would be busy for him.

Once he got inside of his home, he noticed that the lights were dimmed with candles. He noticed a note on the table that read: *Follow the candles!* Fabian smiled, then walked the trail of the candles, which led up to his bedroom. He noticed Fancy dressed in a short silk robe with her hair pinned up. She sat with her legs crossed and with a glass of wine in her hand.

"I see you finally made it home," she said lustfully.

"Yep," he said with a grin.

Fancy was very pretty with gorgeous chocolate skin. Fabian had a thing for chocolate girls. With her round, brown eyes and kissable lips, she knew she was nothing short of fine. Her body was the highlight, with wide hips and an ass like a horse; it was the first thing Fabian saw when they met. Fancy sauntered over to Fabian, where she dropped to her knees and pulled out his massive love stick. Fabian licked his lips in anticipation of seeing her slobbin' on his dick. Her small, manicured fingers looked so sexy stroking him up and down.

"How much have you missed me?" Fancy asked.

"He'll tell you," Fabian said pointing at his dick.

Fancy blew on the tip, then began to deep throat his shaft. Fabian bit his bottom lip to keep from screaming out loud. Fancy was hands down the best at giving head.

Fabian could feel his nut building up, so he grabbed the back of Fancy's head and pulled her back.

"Turn that ass around," he demanded.

Fancy turned around at lightning speed. She knew Fabian was about to blow her back out and couldn't wait to yell out his name. He hurried and put on a condom, then rammed his dick into Fancy's wet opening. Fancy clenched the sheets as Fabian found her spot.

"Baby, that's my spot," Fancy whined.

Fabian didn't respond as he gripped her hips, going all the way in. He was going so deep that he was trying to hit her cervix. Soon after, Fancy's walls began to contract as her cum flowed like the Beaver Dam River. He pulled out and saw that the condom was coated with her juices. He hurried and slid back into her wet pussy, picking up his pace. Fabian tried to hold on, but couldn't and shot loads of semen into the condom. After his toe curling orgasm, Fabian slowly pulled out of Fancy and went to shower. After cleansing himself and throwing on some boxers, he got under the covers ready for sleep.

"Fabian, I don't think Braylon is doing a good job at managing you," Fancy said.

"Why is that?" Fabian asked with his eyes closed.

She positioned herself towards him before replying. "Because you should be doing way more promoting than you're doing. You need to be on a promotional tour," Fancy stated.

Fabian released a deep sigh as he listened to Fancy ramble on about his career. She was always trying to tell him what he should do with his business. She even criticized his brother, which he despised because he loved his brother so much. Most times, Fabian would just let her talk, but he was really getting annoyed with her unsolicited opinions.

"Listen, I don't need you telling me about my career. Braylon is holding it down *as usual*," Fabian quipped.

Fancy scoffed. "Yeah, he's holding it down alright. And why does he get twenty percent instead of fifteen?"

"Because that's what I want to give him. I make sure all of my family eats good, including your good shopping ass. So stay in your place, shit," he shot.

"Stay in my place?" Fancy repeated appalled.

"Yeah, stay in your place."

Fancy shot him a look filled with rage, then got up and went to the guest bedroom. Fabian always said things like that to hurt her feelings. She wasn't trying to run his life. She was only trying to make suggestions that would heighten his career. But, as usual, Fabian always took it the wrong way and said something off the wall.

CHAPTER 3

Fancy cruised the streets of downtown Milwaukee in her brand new BMW. She knew she was a bad chick, and no one could tell her differently. She was confident and cocky, all wrapped in one. Fancy took being Fabian's wifey very serious. That's why she made sure everything was tight, from her Malaysian textured hair down to her French-tip toenails.

Fancy was still pissed at Fabian for their argument from the other night, but she let it go since he was on the road. She always got excited when Fabian left because that meant she could spend as much money as she wanted to.He always tried to give her a budget to stay within when he left, but she always exceeded that. Fancy loved Fabian but loved his money more. When they had met at that industry party, she was on a mission to snag herself a baller but lucked up when she bumped into Fabian. Fabian radiated a confidence so strong that he commanded everyone's attention in the room. After one date and her famous head game, she knew Fabian was hooked.

"Hello," Fancy answered, as her ringing cell phone interrupted her reverie.

"How are you?" the deep voice asked.

Fancy inhaled deeply. "I'm doing okay. How about you?" she asked knowing exactly who the caller was.

"It depends on what you tell me. You took care of that yet?"

Fancy stalled. "Um…Not yet. I need a little bit more time."

"Well, you know time waits for no man. I need that done as soon as possible, or we're going to have some situations," he declared and hung up.

Fancy sighed and threw her phone in the back seat. It was time for her to make some moves that would benefit her, but it wasn't gonna be easy.

She pulled up to a hotel located near the airport and got out. She checked in at the desk and was given a key. After a ride on the elevator, Fancy walked to the door and stuck her key in. She opened the door and was greeted by her side piece, Evan. He was white and Puerto Rican with short hair and a goatee.

Fancy had met Evan a year ago when she attended a Bucks game. They began their affair shortly after they met. Evan was aware that Fancy was in a relationship and didn't have a problem with it since he was married. Evan was attentive and caring and that's what drew Fancy to him.

"Damn, it took you long enough. I thought you had changed your mind," he said, kissing her lips.

Fancy smiled. "No, you know I can't miss seeing your sexy ass," she purred.

"Really? So what do you need me to do for you? I didn't like the way you sounded over the phone yesterday. Is he still treating you like shit?" Evan asked as he wrapped his arms around her waist.

Fancy had lied and told Evan that Fabian was this crazed individual who verbally and physically abused her, so she sighed and replied, "Of course he is, but I don't want to talk about him. I could really use your tongue right now." She smiled.

"Get naked."

****

Kylie sat peacefully on her balcony while sipping on a glass of Pinot Grigio. She owned a loft in Downtown Milwaukee that sat along Lake Michigan. Most nights, Kylie would sit and watch the sunset, which was her therapy. Nothing else mattered when Kylie got lost in her thoughts. Most times, she would think about her mother, who she lost to cancer three years prior. When her mother went on to be with the Lord, Kylie had never experienced a pain so great. She was her best friend and confidante, and to lose her was like a gunshot to the heart.

When her mother died, Kylie buried herself in her work trying to block the pain that lay within. She made sure her days consisted of nothing but fashion and decision-making. Most days felt like a blur to her because she didn't know if she was coming or going. With the strength of God and antidepressants, Kylie was making it through. If only she could put a remedy together to heal her broken heart, her life would be great.

Kylie's last relationship had mentally drained her. Everything had started well between her and Dario. He was an aspiring artist with big dreams. The two fell in love with each other as the months passed. After a year and a half of being with Dario, Kylie was almost certain that she had found her husband, until he hit her with some devastating news: he couldn't handle her career. Kylie was hurt, to say the least, but wasn't in the business of chasing men, so she tried to move on. But two weeks later, Kylie found out that she was six weeks pregnant with Dario's child. She took the news well, but was on pins in needles anticipating his reaction. Once she told him, he flipped out, saying that he wasn't ready to be a father. He even suggested that she get an abortion. Once again, Kylie had been crushed by the man she truly loved.

Declaring that day that she didn't need Dario, Kylie decided to carry her child to term, but with the stress of the breakup and lack of nutrients, Kylie suffered a miscarriage. Overwhelmed with grief, Kylie took a leave of absence and stayed secluded in her loft. Her days were consumed with nothing but sleeping and medications.

After a month, Kylie went back to work and got back on her grind. She vowed that she would never let a man knock her off of her square ever again.

The ringing of her cell phone caused her to snap back to the present.

"This is Kylie."

"What you doing, heffa?" Kellan asked.

"I'm sippin'. What does your ass want?"

"I was thinking we should go out before we fly to the A tomorrow."

"I don't feel like it," Kylie groaned.

"Why? You know you have been such a lame lately. Let's go have some fun," Kellan whined.

Kylie smacked her lips. "How many times do I have to tell you that I've done the club scene already? It's boring now."

"Yeah, yeah. I've heard that before, but we have a very busy schedule coming up, and I want to have a little bit of fun with my favorite cousin. What do you say?" Kellan said sweetly.

"Oh alright. I guess," Kylie gave in.

"*Yesss.* I'm on my way to get dressed at your house."

"Okay," Kylie said, hanging up the phone and walking into her room. She opened the doors to her walk in closet and planted her hands on her hips. "What should I shut the club down with?"

****

Fancy parked curbside waiting for Fabian to appear. She insisted on picking him up from the airport so he wouldn't go out with Braylon and his cousins. In actuality, Fancy was jealous of all the relationships that Fabian had with his family. She wanted him all to herself and felt threatened whenever his family came around. They didn't exactly like Fancy either and had no problem expressing it to her; especially his mother, Monet.

Monet couldn't understand why her son had settled for a tramp like Fancy. She also couldn't understand how Fancy called herself a model when all she did was show her ass. His mother summed Fancy up as a money-hungry whore who didn't have her son's best interest at heart.

Fancy honked the horn when she spotted Fabian. She melted at the sight of him looking like an African god. He bopped over to the car, then hopped in.

"What's up, babe?" Fabian asked before kissing her.

Fancy bit down on her lips in response to his kiss. "You...That's what's up," she said. "How was New York?" she asked, pulling off.

He washed his hands over his face. "Busy as hell. I gotta leave again later this week for a performance in Miami. Then after that, I gotta shoot my video. It's not enough hours in the day," he stressed.

"Yeah, I know. You've been such a busy bee. So do you wanna grab something to eat?"

Fabian nodded his head. "Yeah, but slide by Ava's house so I can pick up Kenyon."

Her face dropped instantly. "Why? I thought we were going to be alone tonight," she scoffed.

Fabian glared at her. "What the hell you mean *why*? I ain't seen my shorty in three days. What you on?" he barked.

"I understand that but-"

"No you don't understand because you don't have any kids," Fabian said cutting her off.

Fancy pulled over, then whipped her head in his direction. "Well, excuse the hell outta me for wanting to spend some time with your ass," she spat.

He shook his head disappointedly. "You're an ignorant ass chick, man. Drop me off at my car. I'm not dealing with your stupid ass today. What kind of woman doesn't want a man to spend time with his son?"

Dismissing his obvious disappointment, she responded, "So we're not going to spend no time together?"

"Hell nah. Take me to my fuckin' car!" he demanded.

Fancy tried not to cry as she pulled off. Why couldn't she and Fabian spend some quality time together alone? No she wasn't a kid-friendly woman, but she dealt with Kenyon off the strength of Fabian. She couldn't win for losing with Fabian, so tonight she was going to make it all about her.

After Fabian picked up Kenyon, he swung by his mom's house. Walking in, he was greeted by the smell of tacos, which were his favorite. They walked back to the kitchen, where they saw Monet stirring a pot of meat for her famous tacos. Kenyon ran over to her and hugged her waist.

"Hey, Nana!" he gleamed.

"Hi, Nana's boy. How are you doing today?" she smiled.

Fabian's mom was a spunky, God-fearing, tell-it-to-your-face kind of woman. Monet looked good for her age. To be forty-nine years old, Monet had not one wrinkle on her face. Her hair was cut in a blunt shoulder length cut, she had chiseled cheeks and the same eyes as Fabian.

"What's up, mama?" Fabian said, taking a seat at the table.

"Hey, you finally got some time for ya old lady," she teased.

Fabian playfully rolled his eyes. "Come on, Mama. It ain't even like that."

"That's what you say. Why haven't I seen my grandson in two weeks?" she asked.

"You know I'm in and out of town. You gotta call Ava when you wanna see him."

"Uh huh...You hungry?"

Fabian nodded eagerly. "Yeah. Hook me up."

Monet fixed Kenyon and Fabian a plate of tacos. Before she could sit down to eat, they were already on their last one.

"Well, damn, were you hungry, baby?"

Fabian laughed. "I'm always hungry."

"That girlfriend of yours still doesn't cook?"

He scoffed. "Nah, all she knows how to do is spend money," he spat.

"You sure do know how to pick them. When are you gonna bring home a nice girl with her own job and money? It's time to leave them birds alone, Fabian," Monet warned.

"Man, I know. Fancy is starting to dance on my last nerve, ma. She had the nerve to get mad 'cause I wanted to pick up Kenyon today," Fabian seethed, whispering the last part to keep his son from hearing.

Monet gave him a twisted look not, believing what he'd just said. "Are you serious? That is not a real woman, and I'm telling you, boy, she is nothing but trouble. Has your mother ever been wrong about girls?"

"No, not really," Fabian responded in deep thought.

"Okay then, and don't bring her to my house no more," Monet warned.

"Aight, OG. Calm down," he laughed.

She rolled her eyes. "Call it what you want, Fabian." She then readdressed her grandson. "Come on, Kenyon. Nana made some oatmeal raisin cookies."

Fabian sat pondering. He was starting to get really sick of Fancy's behavior. How could she not want him to see his son? Kenyon meant everything to Fabian, and Fancy knew that. He had begun to look at her in a different light, and the feelings he did have for her were starting to melt away.

"Dad, I want to stay with Nana; can I?" Kenyon asked with pleading eyes.

"How you gonna trade on daddy like that?" Fabian joked.

"Aww, dad, it ain't like that. Can I please?"

"Yeah, man, whatever you want."

"Yes!" Kenyon exclaimed, running off.

Fabian smiled, then prepared himself to go home.

Once he arrived, he was happy to see that he had the house all to himself. He got a bottle of Hennessey and listened to instrumentals from various producers. He let the sounds take him to a place far away. His life was always on a fast rollercoaster. He rarely had time to himself. Fabian's life consisted of studios, traveling from city to city, groupies, photo shoots and living in the fast lane. He was grateful for his success, but at times it was stressful. Most days, he wanted to relax and chill with his family, but this was the life he had chosen, and he was willing to ride it out until the wheels fell off.

While skipping to the next track, he noticed Fancy walk in. She looked like she had been out clubbing, from what he could see.

Fabian gave her a pissed off look, then closed his eyes. He damn sure wasn't going to act like everything was cool. What she'd said to him earlier had raised a red flag for him. If she couldn't accept his son, then there was no point of them being together.

She walked over to him on egg shells. Then she sat next to Fabian, wondering if he was still mad, but by the look on his face, she knew what it was.

"Babe, you still mad at me?" she asked softly.

Fabian glared at her. "Hell yeah, I am, and right now, I don't feel like talking to your ass," he said in a calm manner.

"Come on, Fabian. What did I say that was so bad?" she asked.

Fabian huffed. "Fancy, you have a problem with me being a father, and frankly, I don't see our relationship lasting if you don't want my son around."

"Baby, you know I love Kenyon," she lied. "Why would you say that?"

Fabian looked at her with a mean scowl. "Get real, Fancy. Who you think you talking to? Whenever I bring up Kenyon's name, your ass throws a fucking temper tantrum like a little ass kid. I don't like that shit for real, and if you can't accept my son, then you need to find somebody else."

Fancy had to think quickly if she wanted to redeem herself. He had never expressed to her the idea of ending their relationship, so she knew she had pushed some heavy buttons earlier. She couldn't risk losing Fabian, so she told him what he wanted to hear.

"Baby, you know I don't want anybody else. I'm in this for the long haul, and I do accept Kenyon. What do I have to do for you to believe me?" she purred.

Without warning, Fabian stood up and exited the room. He wasn't trying to hear anything else Fancy had to say. She would always say things but her actions overpowered her words.

Fabian didn't feel like being bothered and went into the guest room to sleep.

CHAPTER 4

"So, are you ready for your appearance on Project Runway?" Kellan asked, excitedly.

"I am," Kylie nodded. "It's going to be fun to judge someone else's creations," she laughed.

"So, while you're there, Taraji would like for you to style her for the NAACP Image Awards, and then you have to fly to LA so you can go over the designs for the jewelry line. That has to be done before next week so they can start on the pieces," Kellan explained.

"I know; so much to do in so little time. I need a vacation for real though."

"Don't trip, baby girl; your hard work will pay off in the long run."

Their conversation was interrupted by a knock on the door. Kylie gave permission to enter and was greeted by Ashlee, one of the stylists that worked for her. Ashlee stayed in the hot seat with Kylie because she was never on time and many clients complained about her. On top of that, she had an addiction to Oxycontin pills, which she constantly denied. There were some occasions where Ashlee would show up to a photo shoot nodding off and incoherent. She had one last chance before Kylie sent her packing.

"Hey, Miss Kylie. Hey, Kellan," Ashlee greeted.

"Why were you late to that video shoot, Ashlee? You put them behind at least two hours," Kylie snapped.

Ashlee put her hands up in a pleading manner. "I know. I got caught up," she said all in one breath.

"What was it? Were you high?"

Ashlee shook her head rapidly. "No, nothing like that, and I promise this will never happen again."

"I know it won't," Kylie said, rolling her eyes. "Because I'm giving you one last chance. You have to style the rapper Fabian for his video shoot on Friday. Mess this up and it's goodbye. Do you understand, Ashlee?" Kylie said sternly.

"Yes, and thank you so much," she said on her way out.

Kellan smacked her lips. "I don't know why you keep giving her crack head ass so many chances," she scoffed.

"Don't trip. Next time she's out."

****

Fabian sat in his hotel room doing an interview with VLADTV.com about his recent success. Unlike traditional interviews, Fabian got to use profanity and say what he really felt about the hip hop scene. He was asked why he wasn't signed to a record company, and Fabian's answer was that he didn't want to be. He felt that he was doing great without a record deal.

Fabian had a bitter taste in his mouth when it came to record labels. He didn't want to become a slave and be stuck in a contract for years. Fabian wanted to be the one in control when it came to his music and his money. He would rather pay out of pocket for promotion than to let a company pay for it and pocket all of his royalties. The music scene wasn't like it used to be. There was too much demonic energy that came from a lot of artists, and Fabian wanted no parts of it. He believed in his Lord and savior Jesus Christ and felt that his talents were God-given.

After his interview was over, Braylon came into his hotel room with a smile on his face.

"Why you smiling so hard?" Fabian asked.

"'Cause we get to shoot your video back in the Mil."

He grinned. "For real? On what?"

"Straight up, and then next week it'll premiere on Tidal."

Fabian rubbed his hands together. "That's what's up. Maybe I should try to get in the studio with DJ Khaled next week."

"Yeah, and Stacks on Deck Records keep hitting my line up trying to get you to sign. They are offering you a million-dollar advance and plenty of advertisement. I told them I would get back with them though."

Fabian shook his head. "Man, I'm straight. I don't wanna sign with a label right now," he stressed.

"Bro, I feel you. I don't want you to sell out either. We'll just keep doing what we're doing and get this money," Braylon stated.

Fabian's phone started to ring in the midst of their conversation. He looked at the caller ID and sighed. It was Fancy calling for the hundredth time. Fabian didn't want to talk to her because she had left a bad taste in his mouth before he left home. Thinking that something may be wrong he answered.

"Yeah."

"Hey," she said awkwardly.

"What's up?" he asked dryly.

She cleared her throat before speaking. "I was in New York and wondered if you wanted to have dinner somewhere?"

"What are you doing here?"

"I had a photo shoot earlier, but I wanted to see you. I've missed you, babe."

Fabian thought for a moment. He wanted to see what she had to say, so he told her to meet him in the restaurant downstairs from his hotel.

****

Fancy arrived a little early just so she could drink her nervousness away. Fabian had really shown that he was disgusted with her, so she didn't know what to expect. Plus, she had to set up something, which had her nerves in a frenzy.

Fabian had emerged from the elevator looking better than ever. His hair cut was on point, as well as his goatee. He sported a black t-shirt, black Diesel jeans and black Giuseppe sneakers.

The only jewelry he wore was a diamond dog tag with Kenyon's face on it.

Fancy stood up as he approached the table. He gave her a quick hug and sat, grabbing a menu. Fancy felt a little salty when Fabian didn't give her a kiss but opted not to start an argument.

They sat in silence for a moment before she broke the ice.

"So how did your performance go?"

Fabian shrugged. "It was cool. I sold out the arena," he said casually.

"How fun," she smiled. "I heard you left with some groupies. What was that all about?"

He glared at her. "Fancy, don't start, or I will take my ass right back to my room."

"Okay, I'm sorry. I just want you to stop being so cold towards me. I know sometimes I run my mouth a little too much, but I love you, and I only want you," she pleaded with a single tear escaping her eye.

Fabian looked into her eyes and felt that she was being truthful. He told himself that if she messed up again that their relationship would be nothing more than a memory. "Stop crying man. You're ugly as hell when you cry," he joked.

"Whatever," she laughed, wiping her eyes.

"No, but for real; stop giving me so much attitude all of the time. I wanna be able to enjoy you, not hate to be around you."

"I know. I'm sorry. I'll make it up to you."

"I know you will," he said with a lustful look.

The waitress brought out their food and they began to eat.

"So what's this I hear that Stacks on Deck Records wanna sign you?" Fancy quizzed.

"That's what I'm hearing, but I ain't trying to sign with them. I'd rather do my own thing, you know?"

"Why not? I think that would be a good move for you."

Fabian shook his head. "I don't. I'm straight."

"I would do it. They are offering you a huge advance."

He glared at her. "How do you know that?"

"I read it somewhere," Fancy lied.

Fabian gave her an unsure look. "I'm really not trying to talk about that right now."

"I think you should think about it. It..."

"Fancy, leave it alone 'cause you don't know shit about the music biz, aight?" Fabian spat, cutting her off.

Fancy resumed eating, but not before she shot him a look that could kill. She was getting really fed up with his attitude and disrespect towards her. He was actually making the decision she had faced easier, and if he kept up his antics, she would do more than what she had planned.

CHAPTER 5

Fabian sat in his trailer preparing for his video shoot. Even though he had shot many videos in his past, this video was different because he would have a love interest. The fact that Fancy insisted on coming irked him more than anything, because she wasn't genuinely interested in his video. He knew she only wanted to come just to keep tabs on him. He was more irritated with the stylist, who was more than an hour late.

Braylon came into the trailer snapping him out of his thoughts.

"Aye, where the hell is the stylist?" Fabian asked.

"I don't know, bro. They're trying to call the company now," Braylon stressed.

Fancy rolled her eyes at Braylon's excuse. *If he would've hired me to be his manager, this wouldn't have happened. Sorry ass Braylon.* "Baby, you want me to go get you something to wear?" Fancy offered.

"Nah, I'm straight," Fabian said, just before walking off.

****

Kylie had just walked into her apartment to grab her iPad. She needed to get back to the office to get outfits together for her future clients. Just as she was locking her door, her cell phone rang.

"This is Kylie."

"Ky, Ashlee didn't show up for the video shoot today. Fabian's people are calling me pissed off, and it looks like you're gonna have to go style him," Kellan said.

Kylie smacked her lips. "I don't believe this shit," she hissed.

"I would go, but I'm at the dentist right now. The clothes should be at the office."

"Okay. I'm on my way. When you talk to Ashlee, let her know it's a wrap for her ass."

"I will. Call me later."

Kylie hung up frustrated. Ashlee was giving her business a bad reputation, which Kylie couldn't afford, so she did what she had to do. She hurried to the office and grabbed the clothes set aside for Fabian. She drove to the video shoot doing about seventy on the highway. Once Kylie arrived at the location, she saw a bunch of people running around like chickens with their heads cut off. She spotted her good buddy, Robbie, the video director.

"Hi, honey," Kylie said walking over to him and giving him a hug,

"Girl, what's up with your people? She's putting us behind for real," he stressed.

"I know, and I apologize, but I'm here, so we good," she smiled.

Robbie smirked at her. "You lucky you're fine, or I would've gone ham on your ass," he joked, eyeing her frame.

"Yeah, I bet. Where's this guy's trailer?"

Robbie pointed towards the trailer where Fabian was and she walked over. She noticed a guy standing right by the door scrolling through his phone.

"Hi, is this Fabian's trailer?" she asked.

Braylon nodded. "Yeah, we've been waiting on you for almost an hour," he stated with lust in his eyes.

"I apologize," Kylie said knocking on the door before letting herself in.

When she got inside, she noticed two men sitting on a couch, then she saw a woman seated next to Fabian.

Fabian stood and then began to walk over to her. Kylie's bedroom eyes smiled at him while his manhood started to grow. He was taken aback by her beauty and liked what he saw. From her loose curls down to her Boutique 9 nude pumps, he liked it all. For a moment, he fantasized how her thick legs would feel wrapped around his waist, and in that same minute, he almost forgot that Fancy was in the room.

"Hi, I'm Kylie. Nice to meet you, and I apologize for the wait," she said, showcasing her pearly whites.

"No problem," Fabian said holding her soft hand a minute longer.

Fancy noticed the flirtatious looks that Fabian was giving and decided to intervene. "We've been waiting for like two hours," she scoffed. "Can you just show the outfits, please?" she snapped.

Kylie decided to smile instead of clap back at the rude woman. She was a professional and planned to handle herself as one. Plus, she knew Fancy was feeling a little threatened by her presence.

Kylie proceeded to line up each outfit on the rack, putting everything in order. She could feel Fabian's eyes on her as she moved from side to side.

"So, here's what I have. Let me know what you would like to wear," Kylie suggested.

Fancy smacked her lips. "I could have done better than that. I don't like it," she scoffed.

Fabian cut his eyes at her. "Aye, chill out."

"That's cool, honey, because I'm not styling you. I'm styling Fabian," Kylie stated sarcastically, before diverting her attention back to Fabian. "Now, which one would you like to wear?" she asked him.

Fabian smiled. He liked Kylie's swag. Most people didn't have the courage to clap back at Fancy, and he dug that.

"Fabe, you don't even rock vests and that blue is not your color," Fancy protested.

Kylie rolled her eyes to the ceiling, fed up with Fancy's unwanted input. "I know that you've been waiting a while, and I apologize for that, but we need to get you dressed so you can get on set. Now would you like for me to do it or your lady here?" she asked.

Fancy snickered. "Girl, that shit look like it came from the clearance rack at Marshalls."

Kylie cleared her throat, getting Fabian's attention. She was done addressing Fancy's ass.

Fabian stood up. "Fancy, can you wait outside until I get done?"

Fancy looked at Fabian appalled that he would even ask her to leave. "You want me to get out because of this bitch?" she screeched.

"You know what?" Fabian snapped. "I tried to be nice; now get your ass out. You're acting too immature, and I don't need that right now."

Embarrassed to the tenth power, Fancy shot up and grabbed all of her belongings. She made it her duty to stick her middle finger up to Kylie before exiting. Kylie chuckled, then waved goodbye to her. Fabian walked over to Kylie and picked out what he wanted to wear. He actually liked what Kylie had picked out for him.

"I think I'm gonna wear this," he stated.

Kylie smiled. "Great, and again, I apologize for the inconvenience earlier."

"It's cool. Don't sweat it," Fabian said, licking his lips.

Kylie unconsciously bit her bottom lip while staring into Fabian's eyes. He was definitely winning in the looks department. Fabian was certainly her type and she creamed at the sight of him. She peeped his swag and could definitely see herself kissing all over his tattooed pecs and abs. But the fact of the matter was that he had a girlfriend... and a rude one at that.

"Okay, I'll let you get dressed. I'll be outside," Kylie said switching her way out of the trailer.

Fabian watched her ass as she made her way out. Kylie was without a doubt one of the sexiest women he had ever laid eyes on. She also had a strong mouthpiece, which he admired.

"Damn, bro, close your mouth," Braylon teased.

Fabian chuckled. "Did you see her? Her thick ass can definitely get it, plus some."

"Man, quit dreaming. Fancy ain't letting that shit happen. You see how she was acting when Kylie was here."

Fabian shook his head. "I know, man. She's on that bullshit. I don't know how much longer I can deal with her childish ass."

"You know I can't stand that broad, man. I put up with her on the strength of you."

Fabian didn't respond and continued to get dressed in silence. He needed to focus on the task at hand, and that was his video shoot.

Once dressed, he hurried out and took his place on set. Kylie walked up to him and adjusted his shirt to make sure that it looked neat. He didn't see Fancy anywhere in sight, which meant she'd caught an attitude and left.

After making sure Fabian looked up to par, Kylie went to stand on the sideline.

Kylie smiled while watching Fabian get into character. She liked the way he moved. He wasn't trying too hard but still made his presence known.

Why am I into this guy like this? He probably got five baby mamas, a criminal record and child support payments out the ass. Kylie, stop playing yourself. You don't want a rapper.

After a fourteen-hour shoot, Kylie prepared herself to go home. It had been a long time since Kylie styled a rapper, and she had forgotten how long the shoots could last. Kylie went to grab the clothes from Fabian's trailer and noticed that no one was inside. She quietly made her exit but was stopped when someone called her name. She turned around and was greeted with Fabian walking up to her.

"Thanks for making me look fly," he said smiling.

"You're welcome. It's my job."

"You got a business card in case I want you to style me for future events?" he asked.

Kylie dug in her purse and retrieved one of her business cards. "Next time leave your pit bull at home," she joked, referring to Fancy.

Fabian laughed. "I'm sorry about that. I'll make sure she's nowhere in sight next time."

"Alright. See you later," Kylie said reaching for her car door, which Fabian quickly opened for her.

Oh, I see we have a gentleman, Kylie said to herself. "Thank you," she told Fabian, hopping in.

Kylie gave him one more look before she put her key in the ignition. She couldn't stop the butterflies that danced around in her stomach if she wanted to. A part of her couldn't wait for Fabian to call and request her services. She wouldn't mind being in his presence again.

Fabian watched her pull off, wondering why he was so interested in Kylie. *I gotta have her.*

CHAPTER 6

Fancy stood in the elevator with knots in her stomach. Her anxiety level was through the roof. Fancy had a meeting with the CEO of Stacks on Deck records, and she could feel that it wouldn't be a good one.

The elevator doors opened and Fancy was greeted by the receptionist.

"How can I help you?" she asked.

"Hi. I'm here to see Gregg."

"Have a seat. I'll let him know that you're here."

Fancy sat looking around the office admiring the décor. She wished that she would've had a drink before she came so her nerves wouldn't be so shot.

Before long, the receptionist led her to Gregg's office. Fancy's legs began to tremor as her feet led the way. She thought about turning around but knew this meeting had to happen.

The door was opened to a huge conference room where it held at least thirty chairs with a huge mahogany wooden table. Gregg sat at the end with a glass of liquor in his hand. Fancy slowly made her way over and sat next to him. Gregg didn't say anything to her, which caused Fancy's fear to triple. He sat quietly and sipped on his glass of cognac.

After what seemed like forever, Gregg finally broke the silence. "Fancy, tell me why I don't have my new artist that was promised to me?" he asked, not giving her eye contact.

"I just need a little more time."

"Your time has run out, my dear," he said harshly.

"Gregg, hear me out. Fabian has been extremely busy, and I haven't had the time to talk about the deal," she lied.

"That's not my problem. You shouldn't have taken my money if you knew he wouldn't have time. You assured me that you would get him to sign and that was over two months ago. Now I'm going to give your ass a week to get this done. If it ain't done within the week, you and I are going to have some deadly problems. Now get out of my office."

****

Fancy sat in her bedroom thinking of ways to get Fabian to sign with Stacks on Deck Records. The fact that Fancy took a large sum of money from Gregg made everything much more complicated. Fancy and Gregg had been plotting for months on how to get Fabian to sign with the company. If she was to get him to sign, Gregg promised her a certain percentage of Fabian's future albums. He'd also offered her an advance. She couldn't afford to turn down a deal like that so she agreed.

Gregg wanted Fabian on his label because he knew he would be a cash cow. Fabian was hot right now, and Gregg wanted to jump on his money train. Fancy ensured him that Fabian would be signed to his label by the end of the week, and that was almost two months ago. She was in deep trouble and couldn't help but wonder what would happen to her if she didn't deliver.

Fancy got up, then went to the kitchen to retrieve a snack. On her way back upstairs, she heard the doorbell. Looking through the peephole, she noticed Ava and Kenyon standing there. She opened the door reluctantly.

"Hey, is Fabian here?" Ava asked.

"No, he's not," Fancy answered smugly.

"Well, he told me to drop Kenyon off here so he could take him to school. I have to be at work in like thirty minutes."

Fancy smacked her lips. "Well, I suggest you call him because I'm not doing it," she said, closing the door.

She never liked Ava, so she wasn't about to do her any favors. She couldn't stand the fact that Fabian would always give Ava anything she asked for either.

On the other side of the door, Ava stood appalled. She couldn't believe Fancy had actually disrespected her and slammed the door in her face. Ava hurried and took out her cell phone to dial Fabian's number.

"Hello."

"Fabian, you better check your whore. This bitch just closed the door in me and Kenyon's face!" Ava snapped.

"What?" he asked, not believing her words.

"Like for real, I feel like whooping her ass right now. I have to be at work, and Kenyon needs to get to school."

"I forgot you asked me to take him. Just take him to my mom's, aight? Don't worry about Fancy."

"Yeah okay."

Fabian quickly hung up with Ava and dialed Fancy's number. After being sent to the voicemail four times, he decided to give up. Furious beyond belief, Fabian booked him a flight home so he could deal with Fancy face-to-face.

Braylon came in wondering why Fabian was packing his bags.

"What up, bro? Where you goin'?"

Fabian shook his head. "Man, I gotta take care of something back at home."

"What is it?"

"This bitch Fancy just slammed the door in my son's face, and then she's disrespecting Ava like she ain't shit. I'm damn near about to whoop her ass," he seethed.

Braylon gave him a surprised look. "For real? Yeah, man; go take care of that."

"I am. Reschedule everything for me, and tell them it was a family emergency."

"I got you."

Hours later, Fabian stormed into his house, fresh from his flight. He looked on the lower level for Fancy before heading upstairs. When he got to his bedroom, he saw Fancy stretched out on the chaise getting some beauty sleep.

Fabian walked over to her and shook her roughly.

"Fancy, get up," he demanded.

She began to stretch, and then she finally opened her eyes. "Hey, babe. How was your show?" she asked, oblivious to his tone.

"Fuck that! Why are you disrespecting my son and his mother? What the fuck is your problem?" he yelled.

Fancy sat up straight. "Ava was getting slick with me, and I wasn't about to stand there and listen to her bullshit. I can't help it if your son was with her," she lied.

Fabian gave her a dirty look. "Man, that shit doesn't even sound valid. Why would she get slick with you?" he barked.

"So you're calling me a liar?" she asked standing up.

"Hell yeah, you're lying, and even if she did get slick with you, why the fuck would you slam the door while my son standing there, huh? Did you think I was gon' let that shit slide?"

"Why the fuck would I lie to you? Ava been jealous of our relationship, so yes she had every reason to get slick with me," Fancy reasoned.

Fabian rubbed his temples. "Aye, this right here ain't gon' work. I'ma need you to look for another place to live," he said.

Fancy could feel all of the air escape her lungs. She couldn't believe that Fabian just kicked her out. "Fuck you! I'll leave right now! I don't have to stay here and put up with this bullshit!" Fancy yelled, as she stormed into their closet taking out her luggage.

"I can't believe you, Fabian," she cried bursting into tears.

Fabian rolled his eyes. "Bitch, cut the bullshit out. This has been a long time coming, and you're too immature to ever be the woman I need."

Fabian sat on the bed and made sure Fancy left nothing behind. Fancy kept coming back in to make sure she got everything, but in reality she was hoping Fabian would change his mind. She really didn't see this coming, and she could tell that his mind was made up.

After the fifth time of pretending like she had forgotten something, Fabian snapped out. "Yo, you got everything! Now get your dumb ass out!"

"You know what, Fabian? You're whack and your music is worse! Don't call me no more, bitch," she shouted, then picked up a candle that was on the dresser and threw it at him.

Fabian dodged the candle and began to walk toward Fancy. "Aye, you throw something at me again and watch me slap the fuck out of you!"

Fancy rolled her eyes and grabbed her suitcase. She left out of the room with tears in her eyes. Fancy wanted so desperately to go back and beg for Fabian's forgiveness, but her pride wouldn't let her. She figured she would give him some time to cool off and then try to apologize.

CHAPTER 7

Kylie sat with a blank look on her face. She was tired and in need of a bath. She had been styling a photo shoot for Vogue magazine.

Lately, Kylie had been from city to city working like a Hebrew slave. She promised herself that she would schedule herself an off day with nothing but relaxation. On top of that, Kylie couldn't get her mind off of Fabian. It had been almost a month since his video shoot, and she still thought of him daily. Kylie thought that Fabian would've reached out to her by now, but he hadn't and that left her puzzled. She was hoping that she'd made up for Ashlee's tardiness with her great sense of style.

Fabian's good looks and irresistible charm had pulled her in. Everything about him screamed heartbreaker, but Kylie couldn't help it that she wanted to get to know him a personal level.

After collecting all of the clothing from the shoot, she hopped in her car and took her heels off. As soon as Kylie cranked her engine her cell phone rang.

"Hello," she answered.

"Eww, don't you sound ugly," Kellan joked.

"What do you want? I'm extremely tired."

"I called to see if you wanted to go to The Shrine tonight?"

"In the Chi?" Kylie quizzed.

Kellen popped her lips. "Yeah. Where else?"

Kylie shook her head. "Hell nah. I ain't trying to go to Chicago. Plus, I don't want to get popped either," she fussed.

"Okay, the crime rate *is* a little high, but we'll be safe. Come on, Kylie. I heard it was a big event, and you know we need to network."

Kylie sighed out loud because she knew Kellan was telling the truth, but she honestly didn't have the energy to do anything besides sleep.

"Can we network some other time?" Kylie whined.

"No, ma'am. I'll be at your house around eight."

Kylie hung up, then hurried home. Instead of taking a bath, she decided to take a shower since the time was now seven o'clock. After doing her makeup and flat ironing her hair, she got dressed. She sported an orange blazer with a fishnet corset and black shorts. For her footwear, she sported her black platform Versace booties. After checking her appearance for the third time, Kellan texted Kylie to inform her that she was outside. Kylie grabbed her clutch and shot out of the door.

"Hey, you look gorge as usual," Kellan complimented her as she got inside of the car.

Kylie smiled. "Thank you. Let's do this because I ain't tryin' to be out all night," she warned.

"Alright, shit. Sit your crabby ass back," Kellan joked.

Kellan hit the highway while Kylie took the time to go over her schedule and jewelry line. Before she knew it, they had arrived within an hour and a half. Before getting out of the car, the girls touched up their lipstick. After that was done, they hopped out and strutted to the door bypassing the line.

The Shrine was one of the hottest clubs in the Chicago area so it was packed. Kellan and Kylie walked over to the outside deck and grabbed a seat.

"What event is this?" Kylie asked Kellan.

"I heard it was an industry party."

Kylie shrugged her shoulders and bopped to the music. The DJ was pumping Meek Mill's "Monster". Feeling parched, Kylie made her way to the bar. After waiting for ten minutes, Kylie finally got the bartender's attention. Once she placed her order, she stood checking out the scene.

"Aye, my man, let me get some more bottles in VIP," Kylie heard a man say.

She looked to her right and felt her heart rate speed up. Fabian stood next to her looking like a million-dollar model. He donned a tan-colored button up shirt with some dark denim Armani Exchange jeans and dark denim Lanvin sneakers. His hair cut was immaculate as always and Ray Ban shades shielded his eyes.

"Here you go, beautiful," the bartender said handing her the drinks.

Fabian looked to see who the bartender was referring to and was super surprised to see Kylie standing there looking sexier than a Victoria's Secret model.

"So you ain't gon' speak?" Fabian teased.

Kylie looked at him. "Oh, hey. How are you doing?" she asked, pretending as if she didn't see him.

Fabian licked his lips. "Right now I'm doing better seeing you," he flirted.

Kylie blushed at his comment and struggled to keep her composure. If she stood there any longer, there was no telling what she would be capable of doing.

"Well, it was nice seeing you again." Kylie tried to walk off, but Fabian quickly grabbed her and turned her to face him.

"Why are you running? You with your man or something?" he asked inches away from her face.

Kylie shook her head. "No. My cousin is waiting for me, that's all."

Fabian smiled. "Come chill with us in VIP, and I ain't taking no for an answer."

Kylie nodded. "Okay, I'll be there."

She walked back over to Kellan and handed her the drink.

"Fabian wants us to come chill with him in the VIP," Kylie told her.

Kellan gave her a surprised look. "*The rapper*?"

"Yes, girl. Who else?"

"Hell yeah! Let's go!"

Kylie led the way to the VIP area and was greeted by a bouncer. After telling him her name, he let them through. Fabian got up and walked over to her. Kylie did introductions between him and Kellan, then the girls followed behind him, and he in turn introduced them to his team. Kellan had already had her eyes on Braylon, who looked a lot like Fabian, just with different hair. He wore his hair in a cut with the sides cut into a fade.

The girls each took seats between the guys who were popping bottles left and right.

"Hold up. Where is the pit bull?" Kylie joked.

Fabian laughed. "That's funny. Actually, we broke up like a month ago."

Kylie twisted her lips as if to say he was lying. "I bet. How convenient?"

"True story; no lies," he assured her.

"Okay, I believe you. What you doin' in the Chi?" she asked him.

Fabian took a sip of his drink before answering her. "I had a show earlier. Then, of course, I had to show up here. You know the business, Miss Kylie Brooks," he smiled.

"I see you did your homework," she smirked

He nodded his head. "Since you told my 'pit bull' to Google you, I took it upon myself to see what you were about. I see you though. I'll give it to you; you're fly."

"Thanks," she smiled coyly.

"What are *you* doin' here in the Chi?" he asked her.

"Just hanging out. My cousin begged me to come, and since the drive from Milwaukee to Chicago isn't that far, I agreed."

Fabian nodded. "You're from there, right?"

Kylie nodded. "Yes, I'm from there."

"Me too. It's a small world."

"I know, right?"

Kellan leaned over to Kylie's ear whispering how cute Braylon was. She laughed at Kellan's remarks and sipped on her drink. Kylie had checked Braylon out on the sly and agreed that he was definitely a cutie.

"So what I gotta do for you to become my personal stylist?" Fabian asked.

Kylie released a sigh. "To be honest, I don't have the time, but I can refer you to someone else."

"Nah, I really want you," Fabian stated lustfully.

Kylie smiled feeling the goose bumps run up and down her arms. She didn't know what it was about Fabian that made her want to change her last name to his.

After hours of partying with Fabian's crew, the girls called it a night. Fabian walked Kylie to the car and Kellan stayed behind talking with Braylon.

"So can I get your personal number instead of the business one?" Fabian asked with his cell phone in his hand.

Kylie giggled. "I guess so," she said putting her number in his phone.

"Oh, you guess, huh? I wanna take you out. When do you have a break?" he asked stepping into her personal space.

She could feel her breathing become shallow as he looked deep into her eyes. "Maybe by the end of the week."

Fabian cupped her chin and kissed her softly. All night he had been wanting to savor her juicy lips. Kylie's lips were a perfect taste as he alternated from top to bottom. She unconsciously wrapped her arms around his neck, feeling her nipples stand at attention. Their tongues danced for a minute before parting ways.

"Damn, who told you to kiss me like that?" Kylie whispered.

"I did," Fabian spoke.

"Whatever," she teased. "Call me."

Fabian gave her a quick peck before opening the door for her. After making sure she was safely inside of the car, Fabian walked off. Kylie sat in bliss while waiting for Kellan to get to the car.

Moments later, Kellan hopped in, amped up talking about Braylon.

"Girl, Braylon is gonna fuck around and make me give him some," she laughed.

"I see. You were all in his face smiling like a crackhead at the crack house," Kylie joked.

Kellan cut her eyes at Kylie. "I know you ain't talkin'? Fabian had you about to give him your funky panties. I ain't mad at you though; he's fine *and* paid."

"You know that don't really get me excited. I'm more drawn to his personality," Kylie stated.

"Yeah, I know. Let's be out.",

CHAPTER 8

Fancy sat in her studio apartment located in the suburbs of Milwaukee. It had been a month since she had last seen Fabian. She missed him terribly and wondered if he missed her. Fancy tried contacting him a couple of times, but he never returned her call. She had begun to regret her decision of slamming the door in Ava and Kenyon's face. Fancy knew that she had gone overboard with that stunt. She had gotten away with so much dirt during the duration of her and Fabian's relationship that she thought he would never leave her. But reality had set in that he didn't want anything to do with her.

Evan had called but Fancy didn't really want to talk to him. She had only messed with him for the thrill of it. Now that Fabian had dumped her, Fancy didn't want to see Evan anymore.

On top of that, since Fancy was unable to deliver Fabian to Stacks on Deck Records, she was forced to work for Gregg. Gregg had given her an ultimatum of working the money off or being hurt physically. Of course, Fancy took the first option. She had jumped head first into the industry and couldn't get out.

Fancy no longer had control of her own life.

To the world, Fancy appeared to be a sexy model, video vixen, but to herself, she was nothing more than a high-priced slave. Gregg made all of her career decisions, down to the time of her breaks. Fancy was definitely living in the fast lane, but had no way to escape. She wanted to run, but if she tried to hide, there was a big chance that Gregg would find her.

Logging on to her computer, Fancy surfed the urban blogs hoping to see some info on Fabian. Not seeing much, she logged off and then went into the bathroom.

Fancy opened her bathroom cabinet and grabbed one of the ecstasy pills that she'd been popping for the last three weeks. Fancy had become depressed due to her break-up with Fabian. She didn't think it would hurt this bad, but it did, and it caused Fancy to rely on drugs to take the pain away. She started off just taking one pill once every three days, then she soon graduated to one every day.

She hurriedly swallowed one, eagerly anticipating the high it would provide her. She wanted the life she used to have but no longer possessed. Fancy was waist deep and didn't know how to get out.

****

Kylie sat in her room doing one of her favorite hobbies; painting. Ever since she was a little girl, painting had been a passion of hers up until her mother passed away. After her mother died, Kylie stopped painting. In her mind, painting was connected to her mother, and when her mom died, so did Kylie's urge to paint. Two years after her mother's death, Kylie began to paint again. She didn't know what made her pick up the paint brush again, but she was glad that she did. Her mother always told her that she should sell her paintings in art galleries. A part of Kylie wanted something that was only for her, so she never showed her paintings to anyone, except Kellan.

After taking a break, Kylie checked her phone. She had missed a call from Fabian, which had come through over an hour ago. Recently, the two had been talking nonstop in between shows and photo shoots. Kylie truly enjoyed his conversation and he enjoyed hers. Although they hadn't found the time to see each other, they both made sure to keep in contact.

She dialed his number hoping that he wasn't busy.

"Hello," he answered.

"Hey. You called me?" Kylie smiled.

"Nah, you just saw a missed call from my number," Fabian joked.

Kylie smacked her lips. "You know what; don't get cute. What's up?"

"I just got off my flight. I'm headed home. I wanna see you tonight. You in the Mil, right?"

"Yeah, I'm home."

"Cool. Let's meet somewhere around eight o'clock. Where you wanna go? And pick somewhere low key so I won't run into any fans," he said

"Umm… Let's go to the Pizza Shuttle. It's Sunday so I'm sure it's not crowded."

"Aight then. I'll see you at eight."

"Okay. Bye."

Kylie decided to take a long bath before her date with Fabian. It had been almost three weeks since their last encounter, and she couldn't wait to see him again.

After her hour-long bath, she did her hair and applied light makeup. Since the Pizza Shuttle wasn't an upscale restaurant, she decided to wear a blazer with skinny jeans and flat sandals.

At seven-thirty on the nose, she was out the door. She hopped in her ride and made her way to her destination bumping Jhene Aiko's "Blue Dream" the whole way there. Once she arrived, Kylie decided to wait in the car rather than inside of the restaurant. After ten minutes of waiting, she saw a black Range Rover pull up and park. A black Escalade pulled up right behind the Range Rover and parked. Fabian hopped out with a big burly man and made his way into the restaurant. Kylie then got out of her car and walked in a little after he did. She spotted him in a booth in the corner with the burly security guard seated at the next table. When she approached, Fabian got up and gave her a hug. She almost melted from his Dolce & Gabbana cologne.

"How are you?" Kylie asked.

"Straight. You look nice," he said checking her out.

Kylie took at seat across from him. "Thanks, so do you. So where are you coming from?" she asked.

"I just left Nashville. Tuesday I gotta head to South Beach."

Kylie grabbed the menu. "You are such a busy man, Mr. Fabian. When do you have time for yourself?"

He shrugged. "Never, but for the important things I always make time. Braylon is kinda good with giving me breaks. What about you? You're just as busy," he said admiring her dark eyes.

Kylie smirked. "I know, and I am getting overwhelmed. Don't get me wrong; I appreciate my job, but sometimes it can become very demanding," she vented.

He nodded. "I understand. Sometimes this lifestyle can take a toll on you mentally and physically."

"I know right, but let's get to this food 'cause I'm hungry. What kind of pizza do you want?" she asked.

"I like pepperoni."

"Eww, nasty. I like sausage, so I guess we have to get half and half."

Kylie got up and walked to the counter to put in her order. Fabian watched as her ass hugged her jeans. Kylie was certainly someone he could vibe with. The fact that she had her own money and career turned him on even more.

When she came back and sat down smiling, Fabian couldn't help but tell her, "I like your smile."

"You're so sweet, "she blushed. "So tell me something that most people don't know about you."

"Umm… I like to read the bible a lot"

"Yeah right," Kylie shot.

"True story. I get inspired reading about the different things that occurred back in that time. I know it's hard to believe, but I do."

"Wow. Not the hardcore rapper, Fabian. I would have never guessed that one."

Fabian chuckled. "A lot of people wouldn't. What about you?"

Kylie rested her index finger on her chin as if she was in deep thought. "Hmm... I love to paint, and I love sports, especially football."

"Word? Hell nah not you. You're too girly for sports."

She giggled. "I'm so serious. I make sure I DVR all of the Packer games," she said biting into her pizza.

"That crack. I love sports too, and I never met a female that loves sports."

"Well, you have now. So tell me; how many kids do you have?"

Fabian nodded as he chewed his food. "One. A son named Kenyon. You?"

She shook her head. "No, I haven't been blessed with any children yet. I can't wait to have some, though. I want a big family," she beamed.

"Me too. I was raised in a big family. My mom has five boys and no girls."

"Damn, really? I know she wanted a daughter."

He nodded. "Yeah, but everybody keeps having boys. I have all nephews; no nieces," Fabian laughed.

"Wow, you guys must only reproduce boys. That's weird," Kylie laughed.

"Hopefully that's not the case. I hope I can have a 'daddy's little girl' one day."

"Hopefully," Kylie said smiling at him.

For the remainder of the date, the couple talked about everything under the sun. Kylie felt like she could tell Fabian her deepest secrets because he was such a great listener. She loved the way he would give his points of view on certain situations without being offensive. Fabian hadn't had a good conversation with a woman in a long time. When he was with Fancy, all she ever talked about was money and negative things, but with Kylie, he could talk to her for hours and actually enjoy it.

After spending hours talking, Fabian walked Kylie to her car. She turned around and faced him as he stared down at her, looking into her eyes.

"You know I'm digging you, right?" he asked, wrapping his arms around her waist.

"I like you too," she admitted, relishing his touch.

He kissed her deeply, causing the butterflies in her stomach to move at a rapid rate. Kylie loved Fabian's kisses. He knew just what to do without overdoing it. They stood on the side of her truck kissing for what seemed like hours before they came up for air.

"What's on your agenda for tomorrow?" he asked, still holding her.

"My day is full, but my evening is free."

Fabian nodded while still looking into her eyes. "Good, I wanna see you before I leave."

"I can make that happen. Call me," she said, giving him another kiss.

He opened her door and watched her get in. She then watched him get into his truck and pull off.

She laughed to herself. *I think I'm in love already.*

CHAPTER 9

Fabian sat on a private jet enjoying some much-needed sleep. He needed to rest up for his upcoming show. He thought about last night and how he had had so much fun with Kylie. The two had gone to Dave & Buster's to unwind and act like big kids. Fabian wanted to make her his without being too thirsty. He also wanted to make sure that he would be available to her when she needed him and not too busy. Fabian had been trying his best not to miss any texts or calls from Kylie. After some of his shows, he would even Facetime her.

Kenyon shook Fabian. "Dad, wake up."

Fabian had decided to let him come with him since he was out of school for spring break.

"What's up, man?" Fabian said groggily, with his eyes still closed.

"You said you would fix my iPad for me. I think it's broken."

"It ain't broken. It's just locked. I'll do it when I get up, aight?"

"Come on, dad. I'm bored," Kenyon whined.

Fabian opened one of his eyes and looked at Kenyon. He could never say no to his son.

"Aight, man. I'll fix it for you."

Kenyon hurried and grabbed the iPad, then sat anxiously by Fabian. Within minutes, Fabian had unlocked his tablet, making it possible for Kenyon to play with it.

"Thanks, dad," Kenyon said.

"You're welcome."

Fabian reached for his phone, checked his messages, and saw that he had a text from Kylie which read: *I hope your show goes well tonight. I can't wait to see u again.*

Fabian smiled as texted her back: *Thanks baby. I'm dying to see you too.*

Braylon came over and sat next to Fabian with his iPad. He tried to peek and see who Fabian was texting. Fabian caught him and said, "Get out my business, bro."

"Who you texting? Ol' girl?" Braylon asked.

Fabian laughed. "Stay out of grown folks business."

"You must be feeling her since you won't tell me. Don't worry; I ain't gon' take her from you," Braylon said with a smirk.

Fabian gave him a screw face. "Now you're reaching."

"Nah, but for real; you like her don't you?

Fabian nodded. "I do. I'm not gon' lie to you."

"Shorty bad, but are you ready to get into another relationship? You just got out of a fucked up situation," Braylon stressed.

"Yeah, but that was almost two months ago. Besides, it was easy for me to break up with Fancy because I hadn't been feeling her for a long time. I stayed with her because I felt sorry for her, and being with me helped boost her little modeling career. But after that shit she pulled with Ava, she had to go. Kylie is different though. She got her own money and career. She's not looking for a come up."

"Yeah, I feel you. I think Fancy scarred us, bro. We definitely don't want you to end up with another one of those," Braylon laughed.

Fabian chuckled. "Nah, never that."

****

Kylie and Kellan were traveling to LA so Kylie could review some pieces from her jewelry line. She was so ecstatic because this had been a long process and to finally see some actual jewelry made her happy.

After their flight, they hurried to the jewelry manufacturer. Once Kylie saw some of the pieces, she was in complete awe. Everything was unique; just the way she had envisioned.

After the meeting, Kylie and Kellan decided to go eat at Katsuya Hollywood, where they could unwind.

"I'm so hungry that I'm starting to get the shakes." Kellan joked.

"I know. Me too. I'm so excited about this jewelry line. It's going to be off the chain," Kylie beamed.

"Yeah it is. You know I want my signature piece first."

"I got you. I have to talk to some of the jewelry stores in Milwaukee so they can be distributors."

Kellan nodded. "Yeah, you need to hop on that. So what's up with you and sexy ass Fabian?" she asked.

Kylie began to blush at the mention of Fabian. "We've been talking a lot lately, and I must admit that I like him. But we haven't put a title on us yet. I'm just going with the flow, and I'm not putting all of my cards on the table just yet."

"I understand, but y'all would make a real cute couple though."

"Yeah, but we're not a couple. What's up with you and Braylon?" Kylie asked changing the subject.

Kellan released a sigh. "We talked a couple times over the phone; you know, nothing serious. He is so busy and so am I, so we never get the chance to hook up with each other. Hopefully when he comes back from South Beach, we'll get to see each other."

"Hopefully. You need somebody to tame your young ass," Kylie joked while stuffing some salad into her mouth.

Kellan sucked her teeth. "Please. You're only two years older than me."

"I'm just joking. How would you like it if you took over the styling business for me?"

Kellan perked up instantly. "I would love that. But are you quitting or something?"

Kylie shook her head. "I want to focus more on my jewelry business and other things. It won't be right away, but I'll let you know," she winked.

"Okay. Let's drink to that."

CHAPTER 10

Fancy sat in her trailer with two other video models. She was exhausted and irritated. She had been on the set since 6am, and it was now going on 10pm. If she had the guts, Fancy would have left a long time ago. Gregg had her cell phone installed with a GPS system which allowed him to track her every move. Fancy regretted ever dealing with Gregg. He had become a huge pain in her ass, and she cursed herself for being so money hungry. Fancy was still missing Fabian and hoped that he would return her call eventually.

While sitting on the couch, one of the girls named Cecilia came and sat by Fancy.

"So what's up with you and Fabian? Is he still ignoring you?" she asked, already knowing the answer.

"What do you think?" Fancy snapped.

Cecelia put her hands in the air. "My bad, *damn*. I think I may know the reason why," she told her.

"What the hell are you talking about?"

"This." Cecilia pulled out her tablet and showed her a picture of Fabian and Kylie getting cozy at a club. Immediately, Fancy felt a flood of rage come over her. She recognized Kylie from Fabian's video shoot. Fancy's heart felt like it had been shattered to pieces after looking at the picture. Fabian looked happy to be in Kylie's presence, and that infuriated Fancy to the maximum.

"That bitch," Fancy seethed.

"You know her?" Cecilia asked.

Fancy cracked her knuckles. "That's Little Miss Styling Bitch. I can't believe he played me for her."

"I know you ain't gon' let her just take your man like that," Cecilia said, hyping Fancy up.

"Hell nah," Fancy sneered. "I will get my man back."

****

Kylie was putting the finishing touches on her seafood pasta when her phone rang. Wiping her hands on a towel she sprinted to answer it.

"Hello."

"What's up? What you doin'?" Fabian asked.

"Just got done cooking. What's up?" she asked smiling.

"What you cook?"

"Seafood pasta. Why you want some?" she asked.

"Hell yeah. Text me your address."

"Okay."

She hung up and texted her address to Fabian. Kylie couldn't contain her excitement as the anticipation of seeing Fabian multiplied. It had been over a week since she had last seen him, but this time would be a little different. This would be the first time that Fabian would be visiting Kylie at her home, and it left her extremely nervous. Since her house was already clean, Kylie hurried and brushed her teeth. She styled her hair into a messy bun and slipped on some leggings.

After thirty minutes, Fabian arrived.

"Hey," she said giving him a hug at the door.

"What's up, girl?" he said hugging her back.

She grabbed his hand and led him to her loft. He was impressed by the décor. It had an artsy feel with an array of colors. First thing Fabian noticed were the paintings that hung on the walls.

"Nice house," he complimented her.

"Thanks. You ready to eat?"

He nodded. "Yeah. You sure you can cook?" Fabian teased, as he walked over to the table and sat.

"You wanna see? Here you go," she said sitting the plate in his face.

She stood next to him and watched him put a forkful into his mouth. He chewed it for a minute, then began to nod his head.

"I guess you can," he smiled.

Kylie smirked. "That's what I thought."

While eating, the couple began to converse about different topics. As they ate, Kylie couldn't take her eyes off of Fabian. He was perfect; from his straight teeth down to his manicured fingernails.

They had finished eating and were chilling in the living room debating about what to watch, when Fabian spoke. "So, Kylie, tell me why a beautiful woman like you ain't been wifed up yet."

Kylie shrugged. "I've never been good in relationships. Usually, I'm the one that always ends up with a broken heart."

"Straight?"

"Yep," she nodded. "My last relationship was the one that made me say fuck a relationship. So I've been single ever since. So what about you? Why did you end your relationship with the pit bull?"

"Shit, it ran its course," he chuckled. "Plus, she didn't like the fact that I had a kid."

"Really? Well, she shouldn't have pursued you if she didn't like kids. "

"That's what I said. How you feel about kids?" he asked.

"I love kids," she responded, her eyes lighting up with a smile at the mention. "I used to wanna work with them, but God had another plan for me."

"I see. So what would you say if a certain rapper wanted you on his team?"

"On his professional team?" Kylie quizzed.

He grinned. "Nah, his personal team."

"Oh, *that* team. I might consider if he promised to be loyal to me and make me a priority," Kylie answered honestly.

"I can do that," Fabian said pulling her close to him.

"Fabian, how are we going make this work? We both have very demanding schedules," she reminded him.

"We'll be aight. If Will and Jada can do it, so can we," he joked.

"I'ma hold you to that," Kylie said, taking him by the face and kissing him softly.

Fabian grabbed her and lifted her so she could straddle him. Kylie continued kissing him as Fabian caressed her ass. No words needed to be spoken for them to know what was about to go down. The feeling Kylie got when Fabian touched her sent electric shocks through her body. She hadn't been sexed in months so she was beyond ready when Fabian removed her tank top. He gently flicked his tongue around her nipples while Kylie bit her bottom lip.

Fabian picked her up and carried her to her bedroom while still kissing her. At that moment, she was the only object of his desire. He laid her on the bed and then removed his shirt, showcasing his ripped physique. Kylie loved what she saw, especially his defined waistline. Kylie strategically unbuckled his belt, letting his jeans fall down to his ankles. Fabian stepped out of them, then crawled between Kylie's legs. He continued to rain kisses along her neck and jaw line. He was making Kylie wetter by the minute as he kissed her on her stomach. He took off her leggings, where he found that she didn't have on any panties.

"You had this pussy ready for me, huh?" he asked her.

Kylie nodded her head as she bit her bottom lip.

The moonlight was the only lighting in the room. Fabian spread her legs apart, then licked her clit lightly. Kylie moaned softly while she toyed with her nipples.

"Shit," Kylie whimpered.

The ecstasy that Fabian was giving her was the most exhilarating feeling she had ever experienced. He continued to assault her clit with his tongue while he inserted two fingers into her opening.

"Wait. Hold on. I'm about to cum," she announced as her legs began to quiver.

Kylie grabbed the back of his head, feeling her orgasm approaching. Within minutes, she came while Fabian continued to savor her juices.

Fabian hurried to grab a condom out of his pants pocket and put it on. He put the head of his dick near her opening while putting one of her legs in the crook of his arm. Fabian proceeded into Kylie's wet pussy, his dick sliding into her tight walls. She was extra wet and warm.

Kylie cringed at the feel of Fabians manhood because his dick was thick. Once her walls were broken in, Fabian began to long stroke her pussy as if it was his duty.

"Shit, Fabian... What you doing to me?" Kylie whispered.

"Marking my territory," he replied.

Fabian relished the feeling of her taut walls around his dick. He was officially addicted to her wet and gushy pussy. Fabian lifted her butt so he could go deeper. He could feel his body get weak as Kylie's wetness hypnotized him. Kylie could feel another orgasm as he attacked her G-spot.

"Baby, I'm about to cum again," she moaned.

"Cum with me," Fabian demanded.

After a few moments, they both climaxed together. Drenched in sweat, Fabian laid on top of Kylie, trying to regain his composure.

He reached up and gave her a sweet sensual kiss, telling her, "It's official; you're mine now."

CHAPTER 11

It had been two months after their first sexual escapade and Kylie had been above cloud nine. She had finally found someone who genuinely cared about her. Fabian was attentive to her needs and desires, which made Kylie fall for him even harder, and his sex was off the charts. She had never been so sexually satisfied in her life. There were times where their schedules conflicted, but they both made an effort to make their relationship work. Sometimes Kylie would hop on a plane and fly out to see him and vice versa.

This particular day, Fabian had asked Kylie to come out and see him while he was in LA. She didn't see a problem with it since she'd already been booked for an event. After a three-hour flight, Kylie hurried to her hotel so she could shower. She threw on something casual but chic. After applying her lip gloss, she jetted out the door. She caught an uber down to the Shrine auditorium where Fabian was performing.

Once she arrived, she made her way backstage to Fabian's dressing room. When she entered, she saw a couple of guys sitting around. Then she spotted Braylon towards the back of the room and walked toward him.

He smiled and gave her a hug. "What up, girl?"

"Hey, is Fabian still on stage?" she asked.

"Yeah, he should be finishing up soon. What you doin' all the way out here?"

"Working of course," she replied as she took a seat.

"That's what's up. Where my baby Kellan at?" he smirked.

Kylie smacked her lips. "Oh please. Now she's your baby? She tells me how you're always playing her to the left. "

Braylon sighed. "It don't be intentional. I just be extra busy."

Kylie playfully rolled her eyes. "Yeah whatever."

Interrupting their conversation was Fabian. He came in with his shirt off, glistening in sweat. He wore his fitted cap backward with a towel in his hand. He smiled once he saw Kylie sitting there. He made his way over to her while talking shit to the other guys.

"Why you over here flirting with my lady?" he joked with Braylon.

Braylon threw his hands in the air. "My bad, homie."

Kylie stood up and gave him a hug, despite his wet body. He kissed her long and deep while cuffing her ass with his hands.

"What's up, baby?"

"You," she replied giving him another kiss.

"I'm glad you came to see me. What you wanna do tonight?" he asked.

She shrugged. "Umm, it doesn't matter. I'm down for anything."

"Aight. Let me go change real fast."

A short while later, Fabian reemerged looking fresh to death and ready to go. But before they could leave, a girl approached Fabian smiling, which caused Kylie to instantly pick up on her flirtatious behavior.

"I need you for a quick second," the girl told him with a seductive look on her face. She didn't bother to introduce herself to Kylie, which Kylie found rude.

"Aight. Here I come."

Fabian turned to Kylie and assured her that he would be right back. He kissed her on the cheek, then followed the chick out of the door. Kylie sat back down, a little annoyed by the interaction. She helped herself to some refreshments while waiting.

Soon a minute turned into ten minutes and then that turned into thirty minutes. Feeling played, Kylie got up and walked out of the room in search for Fabian. Kylie didn't see Fabian or Braylon around.

This dude got me fucked up! Kylie ranted to herself as she left. She was so pissed off that her face turned red.

Once she arrived back at the hotel, Fabian called her. She ignored his call, then proceeded to call for room service. After she placed her order, Fabian called once again, but this time Kylie answered.

"What?" she snapped.

"Aye, where you at?"

"I left since your ass had me waiting on you for almost forty minutes. So go back and talk to that rude bitch you were with," she spat.

Fabian sucked his teeth. "Man, go head on with that bullshit, Kylie. That was business."

"I don't care. Don't have me waiting on you like I'm one of your groupies. Here I am sacrificing my work to spend time with you, but you wanna keep me waiting like I'm a chicken head," she ranted.

"Are you done? Ain't nobody treating you like a fucking groupie. So what you saying? You don't wanna kick with me?"

"Nah, I made other plans," she lied.

"Bullshit. What hotel you at?"

"I ain't telling you," she said, trying to hold in her laugh.

"Why you playin' games? Come on, baby. I'm trying to spend time with you."

Kylie smiled while still trying to be mean. Truth be told, she still wanted to see him. "I'm at the Wilshire Grand."

"Aight. I'm on my way."

Kylie hung up, then checked some emails, called Kellan and ate her food. Fabian asked for her room number via text, and within minutes, he was knocking on her door.

Kylie opened the door still visibly upset.

"Turn that frown upside down," Fabian teased.

"Ha. Not funny," she snapped while walking off.

Fabian caught up to her and turned her around to face him. "Why you still trippin'? I told you she was talking to me about business."

"Yeah, and her flirty ass looked like she wanted to whip your dick out and suck it right in my face."

"Man, she wasn't flirting with me. You just paranoid," he said waving her off.

Kylie rolled her eyes. "Yeah okay," she said sarcastically.

"Is this what you gon' be on all night? 'Cause if it, is I'ma go back to where I was," Fabian told her.

Kylie wondered if she should remain stubborn or let it go. She really did miss him and wanted to spend time with him, so she let it go.

"I'm sorry for trippin' like that, but don't keep me waiting no more," she warned.

Fabian pulled her close to him. "I promise I won't, Queen Kylie. Now what's up with that?" he asked, while pointing to her camel toe.

Kylie bit her lip. "I don't know. You tell me."

"Shit, you know what I'ma say," he said while kissing and biting on her neck.

She smiled. "I'm starting to think you only like me for my body."

"Stop it. You already know what's up. I can't help it if I'm addicted."

Kylie continued to kiss him softly as his hands roamed all over her ass. Each touch that Fabian delivered to Kylie made her body tingle. Just as Fabian was pulling off her top, his phone rang. Grabbing it out of his pocket, he answered it while still kissing Kylie.

"What up?... I forgot, bro... Do I have to? Aight. I'm on my way." He hung up the phone with a sigh.

"You feel like partying with me for like an hour?" he asked Kylie.

Kylie nodded. "Yeah, but right here where we are," she panted trying to take off his shirt.

"No, I gotta make an appearance at this club. I want you to come with me, and then after we can come back here."

Kylie stopped for a minute, then looked towards the ceiling. She really didn't feel like going to a club, but she didn't want to disappoint Fabian, so she reluctantly agreed.

"I know you don't wanna go, but I want you with me," Fabian said.

"Okay...You're welcome," she smiled.

****

After over a month of talking, Kellan and Braylon had finally made time to see each other. They were sitting at a restaurant on their first date.

"So how was your week?" Kellan asked as she took a sip of her wine.

"That shit was hectic. I'm sure your big head ass had the same week," he joked.

Kellan laughed and then put her middle finger up. "You're gonna stop talking about my damn head."

"I'm just fucking with you," Braylon said as he stared at her.

She was so beautiful to him. Kellan's long legs were screaming to be held in the crook of his arms. Her skin was the shade of sand paper with short hair. She possessed almond shaped eyes with chiseled cheeks. She had perfect bone structure, and in his opinion, she was model-perfect.

"So when was your last relationship?" she asked him.

Braylon shrugged. "A long ass time ago. I really don't have time to be in a relationship, but your cute ass is making me reconsider." He ended with a grin.

Kellan could feel her heart palpitate at his words. "Braylon, you seem like the type that fucks a lot of bitches, and I'm not cut out for that kind of shit."

"The type, huh?" he asked, putting food in his mouth. "I don't fuck around with a lot of women, but I do have needs. You can understand that, right?"

"No, I don't understand," Kellan shot.

"Listen, let's just let shit between us flow, aight? We don't need to be putting a title on us just yet. I'm feeling you and you're feeling me. That's all that matters right now."

Kellan smirked. "You know all the answers, huh?"

Braylon winked at her. "Come here," he requested.

Kellan leaned over and met him in the middle of the table to taste his lips. She could feel her body get hot as Braylon swirled his tongue with hers. After thirty seconds, they reluctantly pulled back.

"Damn, boy. You gon' make me get a room with you tonight," she said biting her lip.

"Shit, we can do that. Don't be scared to give me the pussy," he smirked.

Kellan sat back and thought about the possibility of being intimate with Braylon. She couldn't understand why Braylon was making her break all of her rules. Normally, Kellan would never have sex on the first date, but she and Braylon had been talking for a while now.

She figured she would live a little and pray that he didn't judge her in the morning. "Let's get out of here."

CHAPTER 12

Fancy drove to the offices of Stacks on Deck records. Gregg had texted her earlier saying that he wanted to meet with her. She wondered all morning long what he could possibly want but came up empty.

She walked into the office and went straight to the conference room. Fancy knocked on the door twice before she heard Gregg's voice say, "Come in". She walked in slowly and sat on the chair in front of his desk. He continued his conversation on the phone as if Fancy wasn't there.

Arrogant bastard. she said to herself.

After ten minutes he finally hung up.

"So what's up with you, Fancy? You don't look happy to be in my presence," he smirked.

Fancy discreetly exhaled. "It's not that. I'm just tired," she lied.

"You must still miss Fabian?"

Fancy released a sigh. "Honestly I do," she revealed to Gregg.

Gregg chuckled and shook his head. "Well I'm sure he's not thinking about your ass. Get over him," he spoke harshly.

Fancy rolled her eyes and opted not to say anything. She wasn't in the mood to converse about Fabian.

"Well, I called you here to tell you that one of my artists is nominated for a Grammy, and he needs an escort to the awards show. I want to make him look official with a nice woman on his arm, and what's better than Fancy?" he boasted.

Fancy glared at him. "A lot is better because I'm not doing it," she shot.

"I beg your pardon?" Gregg said with a raised eyebrow.

"Do I look like a hoe to you? What the fuck I look like escorting your artist to the Grammy's? You must think I'm one of them hoes from *She's Got Game*?" Fancy snapped.

Gregg began to roll up his sleeves. He couldn't believe that Fancy had talked to him in the manner than she did. "Did your high siddity broke ass lose your mind? Don't forget you owe me money. You're gonna do whatever I tell you to. To make it clear, I wasn't asking your ass; I was telling you," he barked.

"This is bullshit. I'm out of here," Fancy shot, as she stood to leave.

Gregg grabbed her by her arm, spun her around, and then lifted his right arm and back-handed Fancy in her face. She hit the floor with so much force that she knew she would have a rug burn. Gregg got on top of her, then put his hands around her neck. Fancy began to feel dizzy as Gregg cut off all her oxygen. Her small punches were no match for his strength.

"I don't hear you talking that slick shit now," Gregg taunted her.

Fancy's skin began to lose its color while she still struggled to remain conscious. Feeling as though he had done enough,

Gregg released his hands from Fancy's throat. She lay on the floor crying like a newborn baby and grasping for air.

Gregg fixed his shirt and tie, then walked back over to his desk.

"I'll email you the info. Now get the fuck outta my office," he said calmly.

Fancy got up slowly and walked out but suddenly turned around.

"Wait, listen, if I agree to accompany your artist to the Grammy's, can you set up a gig for me with Fabian? Maybe I could talk to him one more time about signing with your company," she suggested in hopes of seeing Fabian again since he had been ignoring her.

Gregg gave her a menacing stare, then said, "I'll see. Now get out."

Fancy reluctantly walked out and headed out of the office.

The receptionist looked at her and instantly sympathized with her. She had seen a lot of women step out of his office with the same look on their face. As bad as she wanted to help Fancy, she could not risk losing her job. So she watched with empathy as Fancy cried her way onto the elevator.

****

Kellan sat at Caribou Coffee on a short break from her busy schedule. Although her schedule was busy, she didn't mind it because she loved being on the go. To her, it beat being bored. She couldn't have asked for a better career. She loved fashion and to actually become a stylist made it that much better. Being Kylie's assistant was always fun since she and Kylie were extremely close. Though Kellan was a couple years younger than Kylie, they were practically raised together since their mothers were close sisters.

Interrupting her daydream was her phone signaling a text message. It was a text from Braylon apologizing for standing her up on the previous night. She sucked her teeth and erased the message. Kellan was truly tired of being played to the left by Braylon. She thought that after the beautiful night that they shared on their first date that he would become serious about their relationship. But he was all about games, and Kellan wasn't in the mood to play them.

There was no doubt that Kellan was interested in Braylon, but she wasn't willing to sweat him by no means. But whenever she would see him, her compelling stance would melt away in his embrace. She didn't know what it was about him that made her break all of her rules.

After paying for her coffee, Kellan began to walk to her car when she suddenly stopped in her tracks. She adjusted her eyes to make sure she was actually seeing what was happening. Braylon was sitting on the patio of the coffee shop with another woman. Kellan watched him as he smiled and caressed the woman's face.

What the fuck? she thought.

It was not even five minutes ago that he'd sent her a text message apologizing. Now here he was all in another chick's face. She hurried and made her way to Braylon to give him a good tongue lashing but immediately stopped.

What am I doing? This ain't even my man. Fuck this. I'm not about to jump outta my character for no man.

Then Kellan walked back to her car, hopped in and sped off.

When Kellan got back to the office, she stormed to her desk and logged onto her laptop. Kylie noticed her demeanor and wondered what had happened within that twenty-minute break. Kellan had this irritated look plastered on her face.

"Kells, you okay?" Kylie asked.

"Yep," she responded with a slight attitude.

"You sure?"

"I'm cool, aight?" Kellan snapped.

Kylie threw her hands in the air. "Well excuse the hell outta me for caring," she shot.

Kellan decided not to respond to eliminate any argument between her and Kylie. She seriously hadn't been ready for seeing Braylon with another woman. No, they weren't a couple, but Kellan still felt hurt underneath it all.

Conversations with Braylon and the time that they'd spent together kept replaying in her mind, which caused her attitude to adjust from bad to worse.

CHAPTER 13

It had been almost two weeks since Kylie had last seen Fabian, and she was more than annoyed. Kylie understood that he was one of the hottest new rappers in the game and that his schedule would be beyond busy but she was becoming tired of not seeing him. Thoughts of him being with different chicks invaded her mind on a daily basis. It also didn't help that the gossip sites were publishing stories about Fabian being with different groupies.

Kylie wanted to trust Fabian, but when her calls were being unanswered or her text messages being responded to hours later, it was extremely hard not to think negatively. A part of her was still insecure due to her previous relationships. She tried her best not to expose her uncertain and precarious side to Fabian, but it was hard not to.

This particular evening, Kylie was meeting her longtime buddy, Trace, since she was in New York for a couple days. Trace was also a rapper who had several platinum albums and was well known in the music industry. They had been friends ever since Kylie had first broken into the industry.

Kylie walked into Le Bernardin restaurant, heading to the back where Trace was seated. Once he saw her, he stretched a huge smile across his face. Trace was handsome, and his money made him look even better. His skin was the color of milk chocolate. He had doe shaped dark eyes and seductive lips. His goatee with his neatly twisted locs complimented his face. He stood up and gave her a strong bear hug.

"What up, mama?" he asked.

She smiled while taking a seat. "Same ol', same ol'."

The waitress came over and took their orders while Kylie sipped on a glass of Zinfandel that Trace had already ordered for her.

"So I found out you been keeping secrets from me," Trace said with a smirk.

Kylie placed a surprised look on her face. "What do you mean?"

"Why you ain't tell me you and Fabian kickin' it?"

Kylie started to giggle and played coy. "What makes you think that?"

He twisted his lips. "Come on, Ky, don't play crazy. I've seen the pictures."

"Okay, I quit. Yes, we've been seeing each other for quite some time," she admitted.

He shook his head. "Damn, I thought it would always be me and you," Trace joked but was very serious.

"Trace, stop playing. You know you have many options and wasn't checking for little ol' me."

Trace smacked his lips. "Kylie, you know I told you when we first became friends that I liked you, but I let it go because you said you wasn't looking for a relationship at that time," he explained.

"Yeah, I remember. I was just getting into the industry and had no time for that."

"You dissed me, but that's okay," he kidded.

"Yeah whatever," Kylie said sarcastically.

"Nah, but for real; that nigga got you gone, don't he?"

She grinned before replying. "He does, but we've barely been seeing each other since our schedules are so busy; his schedule more than mine."

"Yeah, you gotta remember; he's a hot new artist now," Trace reminded her.

She nodded her head. "I know, but I just wish we could spend more time together."

Trace sat up straight in his seat. "Well, I know firsthand how hard it is to be in a relationship when you're famous. That shit sucks. That's why I ain't with nobody exclusive. But I'm sure y'all will be good." Then Trace reached next to him and handed her a jewelry box. "Here; I bought you something."

Kylie took it, then shook it next to her ear causing Trace to chuckle. She opened it and found a necklace with an iced out heart pendant inside.

"Aww, this is so pretty. Thank you," Kylie gushed.

"You good, ma. That's just for being one of my good friends."

She blushed. "You're so sweet."

For the remainder of their dinner, they ate and laughed about any and everything. Kylie truly appreciated her and Trace's friendship. There were times where she needed things and he was always willing to get it done for her. She had been well aware that Trace wanted more than a friendship, but she didn't want to cross that line and lose a good friend. Plus, she really liked Fabian a lot and was willing to make things work with him.

"You should come out tonight. We're going to the 40/40 Club," Trace told her.

Kylie shook her head. "I don't know. I got an extra early flight in the morning."

"Man, dead that noise. You're coming out, whether you want to or not," he demanded.

Kylie thought about, then said, "Fine. Why not."

Trace told her that he would pick her up around nine. She wracked her brain about what to wear. Fabian had assured her that he would call after his show, and that was over two hours ago. Kylie decided to have fun for the night and forget about everything. She hurried and jumped in the shower. After showering, she styled her hair in a high ponytail with China bangs. Once again, Kylie checked her phone and still didn't see a call from Fabian.

After applying her makeup, Kylie put on her daring outfit, which consisted of a fitted black and white striped crop top with a red Givenchy peplum pencil skirt. For her footwear, she sported black Brian Atwood pumps.

Trace called when he was outside, and Kylie strutted outside looking like she was ready for a night on the town. Trace's driver stood next to the back door that was opened. Kylie slid in and smiled at Trace.

"You look beautiful as always," he complimented her.

"Thanks. So do you."

They drove to the club sipping on champagne while laughing like old times. Trace was always fun to hang out with. He didn't give off the persona of a famous rapper. He was very down to earth and always humbled himself.

Once they arrived, they stepped out of the truck ready to hit the scene with flashing lights and paparazzi blinding them. The 40/40 Club was on ten that night with everybody in the house from Kevin Hart, Rihanna and also Lil' Kim. Trace walked back to his private area where his entourage sat poppin' bottles and mingling. Kylie knew everyone so she didn't feel uncomfortable at all. The DJ was playing all the right music which made Kylie hit the dance floor a couple times. All of the worrying she was doing about her relationship with Fabian had been weighing her down mentally. But now, for the first time in a while, Kylie felt carefree and energized.

After dancing for what seemed like hours, Kylie made her way back to the table. She grabbed her drink and let the cool alcohol coat her throat.

"I saw you out there twerkin'," Trace smiled.

Kylie flicked her ponytail. "You know how I get down," she laughed.

"That wasn't a compliment. You dance just like Mary J. Blige," he joked.

"Boy, bye! I know I can dance," she spat, rolling her eyes at him.

Kylie sat back and checked out the scene. Something told her to look to her left and when she did, her heart began to play hopscotch. She couldn't believe that Fabian was out at the club looking like he was having a great time. He was surrounded by his entourage with a few ladies at his table. Kylie's first thought was to go over and show out, but then she remembered that she was a lady with a successful business and decided to keep it classy. Plus, she was with Trace and she didn't want to embarrass him either.

"Look who's over there having a great time," Kylie said sarcastically to Trace.

He looked over and shook his head with a smirk on his face. "You're not going to go say hi?"

"Of course not."

"Kylie, that's supposed to be your man. Don't be like that."

Kylie popped her lips. "Exactly. He's supposed to be my man, who I haven't seen in two weeks. We're in the same city, and instead of him coming to spend time with me, guess where he is; at a club."

"You don't know the story. It could be business," Trace defended him.

"Yeah okay," Kylie said sarcastically as she stood up, then made her way to the bar.

Fabian bopped his head to the music when all of a sudden he spotted Kylie making her way to the other side of the club.

What the hell is she doing here? he asked himself.

Fabian hadn't heard from her since earlier that morning, so it raised a red flag as to why she would be at a club. Sometimes Fabian hated when Kylie would go out to clubs because he despised when men would drooled over her. She was all his and he planned to keep it that way. But Fabian had been having a difficult time trying to adjust to being this hot rapper in a new relationship. Since Kylie was already established in her career, it made it hard for the couple to spend time together. When he was with Fancy, she didn't have a busy schedule like Kylie, therefore Fabian would see her whenever he wanted. He was trying to balance his life, but it was causing his relationship to suffer a bit. Fabian got up and made his way through the crowd and to the bar. He watched as Kylie stood with her weight shifted on one leg while waiting for her drink.

"What you doin' here?" he asked standing behind her with his lips touching her ear.

Kylie shuddered from his touch. "Same thing you're doing," she shot trying to remain strong.

"I'm getting' money. Why you got an attitude?"

She turned around looking him in his face. "I don't."

Fabian's eyes scanned her body, causing her pussy to get wet. If she wasn't so pissed, she would have run to the nearest hotel so she could get a piece of him.

"Aye, you doin' the most right now," he spat with his finger pointed in her face.

"I ain't doin' shit but trying to get me a drink. You can stop with all that other shit," Kylie snapped.

"Who are you here with?" he asked, ignoring her smart mouth.

"My friends."

"What friends?"

"Trace and his people," she reluctantly said.

Fabian gave her an angry glare. "Trace? Why the hell are you here with another man?" he barked.

"Don't do that, Fabian. Not right now, okay?" she warned him.

"Nah, fuck that. How does it look that my woman at the club with another man? That's not a good look, Kylie. You're giving the gossip blogs ammo to break us up," he seethed.

She rolled her eyes to the ceiling. "Fabian, please. Trace has been my friend for years. How does it look when I haven't seen my man for weeks and when he has the chance to spend time with me, he decides to go to the club? Answer that question," Kylie snapped, staring him down.

"Here you go, ma," the bartender said handing her a drink.

"You know I had to make an appearance here, so don't go there, aight? Look; I'm not even feeling this shit no more. You ready to go or not?" Fabian asked.

"I'll call you when I get to the hotel," Kylie smirked.

"Come again?"

"I'll call you when I leave from here."

Fabian shot her a nasty look. "Nah, you good. Keep your ass here," he said, then stormed off.

Kylie watched as Fabian took off. A part of her wanted to run after him and the other part said to hell with him. That would have been rude of her to leave Trace when she had come there with him. Of course Trace wouldn't have minded, but she still didn't want to do it.

Kylie went back to the table and sat.

"What's wrong?" Trace asked her.

"Nothing," she lied.

"You sure?"

"Positive. Let's go dance."

****

Kylie didn't get back to her hotel until the wee hours of the morning. Her night was filled with nothing but fun, and that was exactly what she needed. Once she got in, she kicked her heels off, then dived head first into the bed. She looked at her phone and thought about calling Fabian. Kylie knew that she had pissed him off, but thought maybe he had cooled off by then. She dialed his number only to be sent to the voicemail. Kylie hung up feeling stupid for reaching out to him.

Kylie got under the covers and tried to drift off to sleep but the images of Fabian's mean scowl kept popping up in her mind. Suddenly a feeling of guilt overcame her.

Maybe I should've left with him.

Turning over to retrieve her phone she texted Fabian.

To: My Honey

You still mad at me?

After waiting ten minutes for a reply, Kylie powered her phone off. A part of her was mad at herself, but then a part of her was pissed at Fabian for keeping an attitude. It was moments like this that Kylie didn't sign up for. She felt like being in a relationship was much more stressful than her job.

So much for making up.

CHAPTER 14

Fabian drove to his mother's house bumping the No Ceilings 2 mixtape. He used the drive to clear his mind and relax. Fabian still hadn't talked to Kylie since she pulled that stunt a week ago. He was still pissed at the fact that she chose to stay and party with another man. He was really questioning his relationship with her. Did he really want someone who gallivanted around the city with different rappers? Even though Kylie and Trace were friends, Fabian still saw that as a sign of disrespect.

Pulling up to his mother's house, Fabian got out and opened the door with his key. He was greeted with the aroma of cooked food. He traveled to the kitchen where Monet was throwing down. She had cooked some collard greens, macaroni and baked chicken. Fabian's youngest brother, Adrian, was seated at the table talking on his cell phone.

"What's going on, mama?" Fabian greeted as he kissed her cheek.

"Hey, baby. Where's my boy?" she asked referring to Kenyon.

"He's at the after school program." Fabian took a seat at the table.

"What up, bro," Adrian said hanging up from his call.

Fabian sat back in his seat. "You got it. What's up with school? You enjoying your senior year?"

"Nah, I'm ready to be done so I can tour with you and Braylon," Adrian cheesed.

Fabian shook his head. "I don't think so, playboy. You have to go to college so you can dominate the basketball scene. Then we can have two breadwinners in the family."

Adrian shrugged. "I guess, man," he said leaving out of the kitchen.

Fabian shook his head, then chuckled. Adrian was forever running after him and Braylon. He loved the fact that Adrian looked up to him, but he still wanted Adrian to become his own person.

"What's up with that dude?" Fabian asked his mother.

Monet shrugged. "You know already. He's smelling his own piss."

Fabian chuckled. "I see. What's been up with you?"

"Working on my future bakery. When am I going to meet your new girlfriend?" she asked taking a seat.

"I don't know. We've been beefin' lately."

"For what? Y'all only been together for five minutes," she joked.

"It's a long story. Let's just say she pissed me off though," Fabian brushed off the subject.

"Well, I got time, so start talking," Monet demanded.

Fabian told his mother the whole story, not leaving out a scene. He always told his mother everything when it came to his relationships. Monet was always honest with him and instructed him on how to treat women.

After telling her everything, Monet shook her head with a smirk on her face.

"I can understand why you're mad, but then I can understand why she is too."

"I don't see how," Fabian shot.

"Because you chose to go to a club rather than spend time with her. I know that you got paid for it, but you don't have to take every offer that comes to you."

"I understand, but how she gon' stay at a club with another man? She basically chose him over me," he spat.

"I wouldn't have left either. You have that bad, when you want something and demand that you have it at that second. And I'm sure that she and the guy have been friends before you came into the picture, so you can't expect her to end her friendship just because you two are together."

"Man, whatever," he pouted.

"No, it's not 'whatever'. It's 'make it right'. You seemed to be really into her, and if you want it to work, you need to put your pride away."

Fabian smirked. "Aight, you win," he said putting his hands in the air.

"Thank you. Now let me make us some plates."

****

Kylie sat in her living room enjoying her girl's night with Kellan and their friends, Ana and Calise. They laughed while playing a game of "He Can Get It". Kylie was still missing Fabian something awful, but she refused to sweat him. With August Alsina's "Been Around The World" playing in the background and Kinky wine being passed around, the girls were feeling good.

"Okay, okay. Stevie J or Lil Scrappy?" Kylie asked.

"Now that's a hard one," Kellan thought out loud.

"Neither!" Calise yelled out.

"Nope, you *have* to pick one," Kylie countered.

Ding dong!

Kylie looked back at the door with a perplexed look on her face. Everyone that she had been expecting to come over had shown up.

"Are y'all expecting anyone else?" Kylie asked the girls.

"No," they all said.

Kylie got up and walked downstairs towards the front door. She was greeted by Fabian looking at her through the glass doors. Her heart rate sped up while he stared a hole into her.

She opened the door and was faced with a bouquet of fresh roses.

"Thank you," she said, giving him a hug and feeling enchanted by his cologne.

She stepped back and checked him out. Fabian looked scrumptious sporting an *I Love Chocolate Girls* t-shirt. He donned some dark Robin denim jeans with high-top Jordan's. His hair and beard were lined to perfection. That night, the only jewelry he wore was his dog tag and diamond earrings.

"What's up?" Kylie asked smelling her flowers.

"I wanna talk to you."

"Okay," she said leading him back to her loft.

Once inside, the girls were surprised to see that it was Fabian. He greeted them with friendly hugs. Once that was done, Kylie excused herself, then she and Fabian went back to her bedroom.

"Y'all having a male bashing party?" Fabian joked.

"Please. We have fun without thinking of men, okay?" Kylie rolled her eyes.

"Yeah okay. But I came over here to apologize for the other night. I know I was wrong for not thinking of you, and I should've taken your feelings into consideration. But I am still salty that you chose to stay with Trace. I almost whooped your ass at the club," he said with a serious look on his face.

Kylie sighed. "Listen, Trace and I have been friends since I became a stylist. There is nothing more to our friendship; just to put that out there. I think I chose to stay just to get back at you, and I'm sorry for that because it was childish on my part. I'm willing to work on our relationship, and I ask that you try a little harder to spend time with me. I know your schedule is ridiculous, but let's just come to a happy medium and do a little more compromising." Then she spat, "And you wasn't gon' touch me."

"You right, and I can do that. Now come here."

Kylie slowly straddled him, kissing him deeply while relishing the feel of his lips.

"I missed you and this pussy too," Fabian whispered.

"We missed you too," she said continuing to devour his lips.

Just as she was getting ready to take her shirt off, she remembered that she had company.

"Damn, you gon' have to wait, daddy," she purred.

"Why? What's up?" he asked.

"My girls are still here."

Fabian sucked his teeth. "Huh? You killin' me. Tell them to take their asses home."

"No. They were here before you came. I got you as soon as they leave," she promised him as she stood up.

"Aight. I'll just catch up on this Packer game," he said grabbing her remote.

"Yeah do that."

"Oh yeah, I want you to come to my house for Thanksgiving to meet my family."

"I'll think about it," she giggled.

"Yeah okay," he said sarcastically.

CHAPTER 15

The day had come for Kylie to finally meet the rest of Fabian's family. Unfortunately, her holiday hadn't been going well since she had spent the entire morning crying. Kylie's mother had passed away the day before Thanksgiving, so this particular holiday was always a sad one for her. She really wasn't up for being around a bunch of people, but she also didn't want to let Fabian down. Looking at her phone, she saw that she had several missed calls. Kylie wasn't in the mood to talk to anyone, so she decided to put her phone on silent. She did, however, text Fabian to confirm that she would still be there to have dinner with his family.

Dragging herself out of bed, Kylie got in the shower and tried to wash away her dreary mood. She missed her mother terribly and would give anything to have her mom in her presence. Unlike most people, Kylie hated the holidays because it reminded her too much of her mother and what they once shared. Sure, she had Kellan's mom, but that wasn't the same. Kylie yearned for her mother's word of wisdom, her smile and also her touch. Kylie wished she could turn back the hands of times so she could be with her just one last time.

After a nice long shower, Kylie put on some makeup to hide the bags that she had accumulated from crying. She decided to wear her hair naturally curly. Once that was done she slipped on her outfit, which consisted of a black leather crop jacket with a long tan and black striped shirt and some black skinny jeans. For her footwear, she decided to keep it casual with some Nike ACG boots. After making sure she looked good, Kylie hopped in her car and made her way to Fabian's house.

Feeling as though she needed some music to cheer her up, she popped in Fabian's mixtape, bumping it the whole way there. Midway through the drive, Trace sent her a text saying, *Happy Thanksgiving! I know this isn't a good time for you, and I'm here if you need me.* She thought that it was very thoughtful of him and made a mental note to text him back.

When she arrived to Fabian's house, she was very impressed. It looked like it belonged on the cover of *Home Magazine.* Once she got out of her truck, a feeling of nervousness set in her body. She had never spent the holidays with someone else's family, so she was feeling more than uneasy. Kylie climbed the steps slowly as her index finger pressed on the doorbell. Moments later, Braylon answered the door with a chicken bone planted in his mouth.

"What's up, girl? You're late," he smirked

"Boy, bye. Fabian told me to be here at three."

Braylon laughed. "I'm just fuckin' with you. Come on. We're about to eat."

Braylon led her down a long hallway to the dining room, which had a long table with the best china she'd ever seen. Everyone was seated, laughing and talking. When she came into the room, Braylon said, "Everybody meet my new girlfriend, Kylie."

Kylie shot him a look, then chuckled. Most of the family believed him until Fabian came in and said, "You wish. What's up, beautiful?" he greeted, giving Kylie a hug and kissing her cheek.

"Not much," she forced out a smile.

Fabian noticed her mood, then took a mental note of it. "Everybody, this is my baby, Kylie. Kylie, this is the family. That's my aunts and uncles over there. Those are my other brothers, Adrian, Tre, with his wife, and Ant. These are my cousins and their wifey's. All the little boys running around are my nephews. And this little dude right here is my mini me, Kenyon." Then he told Kenyon, "Say what up to Kylie."

"Hi, Kylie," he smiled, looking like Fabian's twin. He had the cutest brown eyes with a haircut just like Fabian's.

"Hi, handsome," Kylie greeted him.

Fabian then grabbed her hand and led her to the kitchen where his mom was putting the finishing touches on the dinner.

"Mama, I got someone here I want you to meet. Kylie, this is my mama. Mama, this is Kylie."

Monet turned around and smiled. Kylie was a very attractive young woman to her. Monet was good at reading people and she didn't get a bad vibe from her at all.

"Hello Miss Kylie. It's nice to finally meet you," Monet said, giving her a friendly hug.

"Same here. Thanks for having me."

"Girl, please. You're always welcome here, even if I don't stay here." Monet winked at her.

Fabian sucked his teeth. "How you just gon' invite somebody to my house?"

"Just like I did. Now, the food will be ready in a hot second."

Fabian took Kylie back into the dining area where they sat at the table. Everyone seemed to be in a happy and festive mood. Kylie, on the other hand, was struggling on the inside. Thoughts of her mother remained in her mind causing her emotions to battle each other.

"You look good today, babe," Fabian whispered in her ear, causing Kylie to smile.

After a couple moments, Monet brought out the turkey, which was smoked on a grill. Everything actually looked good in Kylie's eyes. After Fabian said grace, everyone began to pack up their plates with food. Kylie watched as Fabian interacted with Kenyon. It was very heartwarming, to say the least. The sparkle that sat in Kenyon's eyes when Fabian looked at him was beautiful to her.

"So, Kylie, does your family get together for the holidays?" Monet asked.

Kylie shook her head. "Umm, not really. I'm the only child and my mom passed away three years ago. I don't have a huge family."

"Oh, I'm sorry to hear that," Monet sympathized with her.

"What did she die from?" Fabian's youngest brother, Adrian, asked.

Everyone shot him a look, accompanied by the smack of their lips.

"It's cool. She died from lung cancer," Kylie forced out.

Speaking of her mother's death caused a lump to appear in her throat. Feeling as though she was going to break down, Kylie abruptly excused herself from the table. Fabian shot Adrian a looked to kill while he got up to see where Kylie went.

"You talk too much. You never ask a person that question in front of everyone," Monet scolded him.

"My bad mama. I didn't know," Adrian defended himself.

Fabian found Kylie outside sitting on the steps. He noticed the tears streaming down her eyes. Nothing made his heart ache more than seeing Kylie upset and hurt.

"You good?" he asked.

Kylie shook her head. "I hate the holidays," she spoke quietly.

"Is it because of your mother?"

"Yeah, she died the day before Thanksgiving. I miss her so much," Kylie cried harder.

Fabian pulled her close to him and let her get her emotions out. He honestly didn't know what to say since he'd never experienced losing a parent.

"You are so blessed to have your mother. I would give anything just to see my mother again. That was the only person that really loved me beyond my flaws."

Fabian took his finger and wiped her tears away. "Well, I love you."

Kylie looked up at him, searching his eyes for any misleading signs but couldn't read him at the moment. So, instead, she smacked her lips and said, "Yeah right. You don't have to say that to make me feel better."

Fabian smacked his lips as well. "You think I would actually tell you that if I didn't mean it? I'm serious, Ky," he said as he looked her in the eyes.

"I love you too, Fabian," Kylie told him feeling as though a weight had been lifted off of her shoulders. She knew she loved Fabian months ago but wasn't ready to reveal it to him yet. It seemed like every time she told someone that she loved them, they would hurt her to a point where she vowed never to say it again.

"I'm here for you, aight? Don't ever think that you have no one is in your corner. It's me and you against the world," he smiled.

"Thank you," she sniffed

"Now bring your ass. I'm hungry as fuck," he joked and grabbed her hand.

Kylie laughed as she stood with him and followed Fabian back into the house. As she went to the bathroom so she could clean her face off, Fabian resumed eating with his family.

"Is she okay?" Monet asked Fabian, very concerned about Kylie.

"Yeah, it's just that her mom died the day before Thanksgiving, so the holidays aren't a good time for her," he whispered.

"Po' baby. I know it's gotta be rough for her."

Kylie came back into the room feeling much better. After eating dinner, everyone branched off into different areas of the house. Fabian was playing spades with his brothers while Kylie, Monet and Kenyon watched football. Kylie loved Monet instantly because of the way she interacted with her family. Kylie could tell that her family was her life and that she would go through anything just to ensure their safety. She noticed that Kenyon was a very mild mannered little boy. While the other boys chose to run around the house and wreak havoc, Kenyon chose to sit and watch TV.

"Is he always this laid back?" Kylie asked Monet.

"Who? Kenyon? Girl, this is my little scholar right here never gives me any trouble when he stays with me. I'll keep him anytime. Now, them other grand boys? I have to get them only when I get a refill on my Xanax pills," Monet joked.

Kylie busted out laughing at Monet's silliness. She had been cracking Kylie up all night.

"So, Fabian tells me you're a stylist. So you won't mind me calling you to style me for a couple dates now would you?" Monet asked.

"Not at all. Call me anytime. I'll just charge your son," Kylie giggled.

Monet gave her a high five. "Now that's my kind of girl."

Fabian came into the room and sat next to Kylie as he slapped her on her thigh. "What y'all doin'?" he asked.

"Just talking. I was telling your mom that Kenyon is so laid back. I never saw a little kid with so much swag," Kylie said, winking at Kenyon which caused him to smile.

Fabian looked at her with a raised brow. "Do you not see who his daddy is? Y'all should know where he get if from," he boasted.

"Okay, Fabian," Kylie said sarcastically.

He chuckled. "Don't hate, baby."

"Do you hear your son over here?" Kylie asked Monet.

Monet waved her hand dismissively. "Girl, I don't pay him no mind."

"Are you going to stay the night with me?" Fabian whispered in her ear.

Kylie bit her lip and then smiled. "I can do that. I don't have any clothes though. I might have to run home."

"Don't worry about that. I got something you can sleep in, and I got toothbrushes and all that good shit. Just have that pussy ready for me," he said whispering the last part.

Kylie could feel the warmth between her legs once he said that. She couldn't wait for Fabian to fill her insides. "I got you."

CHAPTER 16

Several months had flown by since Fabian had revealed to Kylie that he loved her and he really had been showing her. If he was in town, he would take her to breakfast or take her shopping. If he was on the road, he would send flowers each day that he was gone and also call her after each performance. Fabian had never experienced a love like this and he was enjoying the feeling. He really could see himself with Kylie for the long haul. The fact that Kenyon enjoyed her too was a plus, and she also got along great with Ava.

Kylie, on the other hand, loved the way Fabian treated her, but this eerie feeling that something could go wrong was nagging in the back of her mind. In the past. when her relationships were going good, something would come out of nowhere and break up her happy moment. But when Kylie was in Fabian's presence, she felt complete. Nothing else mattered to her, except him. This was the love Kylie had always wanted, and for that someone to be Fabian made it much more special.

Kylie was getting ready for her jewelry line launch party. It was going to be held at the Art museum in downtown Milwaukee. Kylie had been on pins and needles all day. The anticipation of seeing her own jewelry line had her nerves on ten.

Kellan walked through the door with Kylie's dress in her hand. Kellan looked absolutely stunning in a black lace dress. Her short hair was uniquely styled to perfection and her makeup was applied flawlessly.

"Well don't you look gorgeous?" Kylie sang.

Kellan did a spin. "Thanks, boo. You know I had to show out for my cousin's party."

"I see. I'm scared of you."

Kellan began to finger her hair. "So is Fabian going to be there?" she asked.

Kylie nodded while applying her lashes. "Yep. He should be on his way back from Atlanta."

"Good. Then I can shit on his brother," Kellan smiled deviously.

"Girl, are you still trippin' over him? I could have sworn you were over it."

"I am, but I gotta let him see what he's missing. Any whoo, you better hurry up because the car will be here any minute," Kellan informed her.

Kylie ignored her, intending on taking her time dressing so that she looked perfect. After flawlessly applying her makeup, she did a once over in the mirror.

Damn, I should have been a makeup artist.

Her hair was styled in a high bun, which accentuated her beautiful eyes. That night, she wore a Rachel Pally one shoulder crème colored dress. The dress was very form fitting, showing off her curves. She completed the look with a pair of nude peep-toe pumps and gold accessories. After making sure her appearance was on point, Kylie stepped out and grabbed her clutch.

"You look so pretty, Ky. Fabian is gonna have to keep you by his side tonight," Kellan teased.

"Oh please," Kylie waved her off.

They both left out of the house where a car was waiting. On the ride there, the girls decided to make a toast. Kylie couldn't wait to see her pieces revealed. They arrived within twenty minutes. They saw all kinds of cars parked and guests walking inside of the venue. Kylie walked in, making a grand entrance. All of her guests showed her love, including the singer, Monica, and her husband, Shannon, along with the model, Giselle, and Tom Brady.

The museum was nicely decorated with a brown and crème color scale. Huge ice sculptures were strategically placed all around the room. Hanging from the ceiling were glass balls alongside crystals that created a luxurious sparkle in the room. Last, but not least, her brand's name, *Eilyk,* was propped on the wall from projector screens. Kylie couldn't have been more impressed with the decorations.

Interrupting her admiration was Fabian's mother.

"Hey, honey. This is really beautiful," she said hugging her.

"Thank you. I'm glad you came."

Monet waved her hand at her. "You know I couldn't miss this. Let me introduce you to a friend of mine. Kylie, this is Melvin. Melvin, this is Kylie."

Kylie shook his hand. "Nice to meet you."

"Well, let me go look around. I see some things I like," Monet winked.

"We'll make sure to charge your son," Kylie giggled.

"That's my girl."

Kylie walked away to mingle with her guests. She spotted her good friends from around the way, Paris and Camara. They all attended the same high school and managed to keep up with each other from time to time. Kylie walked over, happy to see them, and gave them a hug.

"Hey, boo. I'm so proud of you. This place looks amazing," Paris complimented her.

Camara nodded her head in agreement. "Yeah, honey, you did that."

Kylie smiled. "Aww! Thank you so much. I'm so glad you guys came. I appreciate that."

Paris waved her hand. "Of course we came. You know you're our girl."

"I see some stuff that would look good on me too," Camara said, eyeing a pair of earrings.

"Ooh me too. We're about to go spend our men's money. We'll catch up to you later," Paris sang as she grabbed Camara's hand and walked off.

Kylie laughed at them and continued to greet her guests. Everyone was in awe of her uniquely designed pieces. She wanted to make sure her jewelry line stood out from the others. Feeling her phone vibrate, Kylie grabbed it out of her clutch and saw that it was Fabian.

"Babe, where are you?" she answered.

"I got some bad news. I'm not gon' be able to make it. I'm still in the A," he spoke.

Kylie rolled her eyes. "Really, Fabian? You promised me you would be here," she whined.

"I know, babe, but I couldn't get out of this shoot. I promise I will make it up to you when I get home," he assured her.

"Yeah whatever. Bye." Kylie hung up with an attitude.

Fabian had really killed her mood by telling her that he wasn't going to be there. She really wanted him to support her, but like always something had come up. Kellan noticed her long face from across the room and went to see what was going on.

"Are you okay?" Kellan asked.

Kylie pouted. "Fabian is not coming. He still is in Atlanta," she said sadly.

Kellan wrapped her arm around Kylie's shoulder and hugged her. "That sucks 'cause I know you wanted him to be here."

"Yeah, but whatever."

"Well, you still have a party to tend to. Don't let that damper your mood."

Kylie nodded. "I know. I'll get it together," she assured Kellan.

Kellan left so she could go mingle while Kylie sat at the bar. She tried to get herself together by ordering a drink.

*It's not his fault, Kylie, s*he told herself. But the more she thought about his absence, it made her angry all over again.

"Why you pouting?" Kylie heard a voice behind her say.

She turned around and saw Trace standing there with his famous smile. With his dreads neatly pulled back and his goatee freshly trimmed, he looked better than ever.

"What are you doing here?" Kylie asked, giving him a hug, pleasantly surprised to see him.

He hugged her tightly, saying, "You know I couldn't miss this."

Kylie smiled. "Thanks for coming. I really appreciate it. I didn't think you would make it since you're on tour and everything."

"I know, but I always make time for you," he smiled.

Kylie gave him an unsure smile, wishing that Fabian had been that adamant about being there to support her.

"Show me some jewelry," Trace requested.

Kylie guided him over to the showcase area and showed him everything. From the look on his face, he seemed as if he liked everything.

"I think I'm gonna get these for my mom," he said, picking out a set of canary yellow diamond earrings.

"That's a nice choice."

Trace began to look around. "Where's your man at?" he asked.

"He couldn't make it. Stuck outta town," she said sadly.

"Is that why you had the long face when I came in?"

"I'm not about to lie; yes."

"Don't sweat it, ma. Look at all of these people who showed up for you. Plus, I'm here," he said eyeing her lustfully.

Kylie chose not to respond and ignored his flirtatious looks. She didn't want to talk about Fabian, so she changed subjects. For the remainder of the night, Kylie had a ball, even though Fabian was on her mind, but she figured she would deal with him later because despite his absence the night was going so well. Kylie had made more sales than she had anticipated. She got nothing but great reviews, which only confirmed that she had got into the right business.

CHAPTER 17

Fabian sat in his trailer ready to knock out his photo shoot for *Rolling Stone* magazine. He was tired and ready to go home but this had to be done. It was an honor for him to grace the cover, but at the same time, he couldn't wait to get home to Kylie. Fabian felt terrible for not going to her launch party. He had tried to get out of the shoot and also tried to reschedule it but there was no way out of it. Fabian didn't want to appear like he put other things in front of her, but his career was in high demand.

After sending Kylie a text message saying that he'd missed her, Fabian sat with his eyes closed thinking about how happy he was. Kylie was everything to him and, honestly, he couldn't see his life without her. Kylie was driven, devoted and intelligent, which was what he admired most.

"Aye, bro, you'll never believe who the model is," Braylon chuckled

"Who?"

"Fancy's whack ass."

Fabian scoffed. "Damn, I don't feel like dealing with her ignorant, petty ass today," he spat.

"I know, bro. Thank God it's only just a photo shoot."

Fabian instantly hopped up and began to get dressed. He went through the clothes trying to pick out something close to fly but everything was weak.

They should've hired my baby to style this shoot. All of this shit is horrible.

Once dressed, he walked onto the set where Fancy stood with this stupid grin on her face. Nothing had changed about her, except her hair color, which was a deep cherry color. She still had a body out of this world. Fabian, being the gentlemen he was, went over to say hi to her.

"What's up, Fancy?"

"You, daddy. You ready to get this shoot done?" she smiled deviously.

"Yep," Fabian replied, ignoring her flirtatious comment.

Fabian and Fancy took numerous pictures. She was being extra flirty with her hand movements while Fabian tried to ignore it. While posing, Fancy whispered in his ear, "I know you miss this."

Fabian shook his head, then chuckled. She hadn't changed a bit, and he was so glad that he had moved on.

After the shoot was done, Fabian headed back to his trailer and began to undress. Hearing the door open, he turned around and saw that Fancy was standing there with a wicked grin on her face.

"What do you want?" Fabian asked.

Fancy licked her lips. "You already know, Fabian. Let's not play games. I want *you*," she stated.

"That's fucked up 'cause you can't have me."

"Why? Because of that styling bitch?" she shot.

"Don't call my lady a bitch. That's disrespectful," he smirked, which pissed her off more.

Fancy scoffed. "Fuck her. You know she could never make you feel the way that I do," she spoke with much confidence.

"You're right. She does it even better than your dumb ass. Quit playin' yourself, Fancy. You and I will never be together again."

Fancy walked over to him and looked him in the eyes. She didn't want to believe that what they shared was something of the past. Fancy wasn't willing to let go and she was going to do everything to get her man back. So she dropped to her knees and quickly pulled down Fabian's sweat pants. He quickly tried to move her hand, but she had already had her hand on his dick.

"What the fuck you doin'? Watch out," he snapped.

Fabian fought to stop her, but when her warm mouth covered his manhood, he had lost the battle. She slobbed on his dick like a pro, taking it all in her mouth. Fancy spit and deep throated his shaft like her life depended on it. The guilty pleasure he was experiencing was almost euphoric. His mind was telling him to stop, but his body was saying he wanted more.

After minutes of toe-curling head, Fabian released his seed, and Fancy swallowed every drop. After she was done, she stood up and whispered in his ear, "I thought she did it better than me," then Fancy licked his ear. She walked out quietly, not saying another word.

Images of Kylie's face invaded Fabian's mind, making him feel a wave of guilt. He swore that he would never hurt her the way her previous boyfriends had. But, in reality, he wasn't any better than the rest of them. If Kylie ever found out about what had just occurred, Kylie would definitely be done with him.

I'm gon' have to take this to the grave.

****

Ring… Ring

The sound of Kylie's phone awoke her from a deep slumber. She tried to ignore it the first time, but the caller wouldn't give up, so she reached over and answered without looking at the caller ID.

"Yeah," she answered groggily

"What's up, baby? I know you ain't still sleep," Fabian said.

"I was. I'm tired. I'll call you when I get up," she tried to hang up.

"Nah, fuck that. I need you to get up and meet me at my crib in the next thirty minutes," he demanded.

"Why?"

"Don't worry about it. Just be here."

Fabian had hung up before she could protest. Kylie willed herself out of bed while cussing and grunting. Her body was in need of some good sleep and just when she thought she could sleep in, she was sadly mistaken.

After taking a quick shower, Kylie slipped on something simple but cute, then hit the door. She didn't even bother to apply any makeup or do her hair, which was styled in a messy bun. After the twenty-minute drive, Kylie had finally arrived. She got out and rang the doorbell. Fabian answered the door in a wife beater and basketball shorts.

"Well, don't you look happy?" he teased

Kylie pushed her way inside of the house. "Shut up, Fabian. I told you I was tired. Now what was so important that I had to be here within thirty minutes?" she crossed her arms over her chest.

"I got a surprise for you, and why are you so tired?" he asked.

"Because I work a lot and was looking forward to finally sleeping in. So where's the surprise?" she asked perking up.

"Close your eyes."

While Kylie closed her eyes, Fabian grabbed her hand and led her into the kitchen. He told her to uncover eyes, and once she did, her mouth dropped open. Fabian had his kitchen table decked out with breakfast food. There was sausage, bacon, pancakes, eggs, grits, fruit and much more. It was so much food that she knew she couldn't eat all of it. Kylie also noticed a large box with a big red bow that sat on one of the chairs. She walked over and lifted the top. Kylie gasped and picked up one of her favorite paintings by Vincent van Gogh.

"Oh my God! Fabian, do you know how much this cost?" she gushed while rubbing her fingers across the painting.

"Hell yeah I know. I started sweating and shit when the lady told me the price," he kidded.

Kylie busted out laughing. "You're so silly, but thank you. This is my absolute favorite painting." She reached up and gave him a sweet kiss.

"I'm sorry I couldn't make it to your party. I really tried to be there. Can you forgive me?" he said holding her tight.

"Yes, since you're about to feed me and bought me this bomb ass painting. You know I can't stay mad at you. Look at all this food. We're not gonna eat all of this."

"I know, but I wanted you to have a selection. Also, your buddy is here too. Aye, Kenyon," Fabian yelled.

Kylie could hear his little footstep coming closer as he suddenly appeared.

"What's up, dad? Oh, hi, Kylie," he waved.

"Hi, handsome. You're hanging out with your pops today?" she asked, giving him a hug.

"Just for now. I gotta leave soon to go to my cousin's house."

"So come on and let's eat before I drop him off," Fabian suggested.

The trio ate and chatted just like a regular family. Kylie loved when Kenyon told his little stories because he sounded so mature for his age. Fabian could tell that Kylie genuinely liked his son and that made his heart smile more. With Fancy, it was always forced, and Kenyon never liked to talk to her.

After eating, Fabian dropped Kenyon off while Kylie waited at his house. She got in his king sized bed and snuggled under the covers. That breakfast had hit the spot for her and she was now drifting off into a good snooze until Fabian came in. He plopped on the bed lying on top of her.

"Get up, Ky. There's no time for sleep. We're about to go," he said tickling her.

"Stop Fabian!" she yelled, laughing uncontrollably.

"Nah, not until you get up."

Kylie laughed. "Okay, babe. Why won't you let me get a ten-minute nap?"

"'Cause we're about to leave. Now get your ass up," he said slapping her on the ass.

Fabian got up and went to throw on some clothes. Kylie still lay in the bed checking her emails through her phone. She finally got up and took her bun out of her hair and let it hang loosely. Fabian came out looking fresh as always. She couldn't get enough of him as she walked up to him and gave him a wet kiss.

"I love you," she whispered to him.

He smacked her ass. "I know."

They left out, hopped in Fabian's car and sped off. Fabian took her to the Majestic Cinema located in Waukesha, where he rented out the entire theater. Kylie felt extra special once again from another one of Fabian's surprise.

"What do you wanna see?" he asked her.

"Um... How about Ride Along 2?"

"Aight."

After receiving their tickets, they stopped to get some junk food and then went into the theater. Kylie snuggled up with her man while feeling like she was on top of the world. So far, Fabian was doing a great job of making up for his absence at her launch party. He was happy that he could make Kylie's day better. When she felt happy that meant he was doing his job as her man. He still felt guilty for the act between him and Fancy, but he wasn't willing to let Kylie go, so he swept it under the rug.

"You love me?" Fabian asked, placing his arm around her neck.

"Just a little."

"Damn, a little? That's fucked up,"

Since Fabian had been surprising her all day, Kylie thought she should return the favor. She quietly climbed on top of Fabian and started kissing on his neck. He quickly reacted and rubbed on her ass. Kylie then traveled to his lips where she covered them with her sweet kisses.

"Take your jacket off for me," Kylie said and stood up.

Since they were in the theater alone, she slid out of her jeans, wearing only a thong. Fabian handed her his jacket, then she wrapped it around her waist. Fabian slid his jeans half way down as he released his pulsating dick. Kylie then sat back on top of him and resumed kissing him.

"Let's see how wet I am, daddy," Kylie purred, sliding down on his thick dick.

Fabian held onto her hips, appreciating the feel of her tight walls. Kissing her hungrily, Fabian grabbed a hand full of her ass so he could control her pace. Her pussy was so wet and moist that he could hear her wetness every time she bounced on his dick. Kylie found her spot as she slid up and down on Fabian's pole. Her breathing became shallow as she felt her first orgasm approaching.

"Damn, baby. Why you so wet?" Fabian asked, feeling his body get weak.

"Babe, you on my spot," Kylie whined, holding him tighter.

Minutes later, Kylie's stomach contracted as her juices rained down. Her body began to convulse violently as she held onto Fabian. He continued to pump in and out of Kylie's gushy walls as he released his seed.

"That was good, baby," Kylie said coming down from her orgasmic high.

"I know, but I ain't finished. Turn around so I can hit it from the back."

CHAPTER 18

After three days of being together, Kylie and Fabian got back to work. She was so ecstatic about the time that she had spent with Fabian. She felt like she had fallen in love all over again. She hated to separate from her boo, but she had to get back on her grind.

She and Kellan were currently on a photo shoot set in downtown LA. They both were styling a video vixen shoot for *Complex Magazine.* While waiting for the models to show up, Kylie sat and texted Fabian her naughty thoughts.

Moments later, the girls showed up, one of them being Fancy. As soon as Kylie spotted her, she sucked her teeth mumbling, "This bitch."

"Who?" Kellan asked.

"Fabian's old chick."

Once Fancy saw Kylie, she grinned, then walked right up to her.

"Well, well, well. If it isn't Little Miss Stylist."

Kylie smirked as she looked at Fancy. "Yes, it is."

"I hope you're ready for me. I'm very hard to please."

Kylie got up, ignoring her remark, then went to speak with the other models. Kellan sat there mugging Fancy, ready for something to jump off. She didn't like Fancy's approach at all and was ready to pop her in the mouth.

Once Kylie introduced herself to all of the models, she presented the bathing suits, which they all loved, except for Fancy.

"All of that shit is whack just like I thought it would be," she shot.

Kellan stood up. "Aye, you better chill out for real," she warned.

"Nah, Kellan, I got this one," Kylie stated.

"You ain't got shit. Take that cheap ass bathing suit that looks like it came from Wal-Mart and stick it up your stuck up ass," Fancy snapped.

"You know what? I'm not going to give your ignorant ass the satisfaction of arguing with you. If you don't like it, that's just too damn bad."

Fancy huffed. "I'll just wear my own shit. You are not about to have me looking a mess. I make too much money for that."

Kylie snickered, finding her last remark amusing. "Last I heard, Gregg makes your money. You ain't making shit. You don't even get a fucking allowance," she shot, embarrassing Fancy.

Fancy glared at her. She couldn't believe that Kylie knew all of her personal business. "Who told you that?"

Kylie smiled, loving the way she had gotten under Fancy's skin. A few weeks ago, she had gotten a called from her college buddy telling her how Fancy had made a deal with Gregg to have Fabian sign with the record company. At first, Kylie was just going to sit on the information and not tell anyone, including Fabian. But Fancy was talking too much shit, so Kylie had to let her know that she knew her secret.

"I have my sources. You're just a broke ass model paying off your debt. Did Fabian know that you were trying to secretly sell him to Stacks on Deck Records?"

Fancy's nostril flared out. "You don't know what the fuck you're talking about!" she yelled, becoming defensive.

"Oh, baby, I think I do. You see, me and Gregg's receptionist are very close. We go way back. We used to be roommates in college, and she gave me the scoop on you, boo. So shut the hell up talking like you're top notch, okay, bitch?" Kylie snapped.

"We'll see who gets the last laugh," Fancy said, then walked out of the room.

Everyone started giggling when she left. The other models were in shock because they had never witnessed Fancy being put in her place.

"Girl, you shut her down," Kellan boasted.

"Somebody had to humble that hoe."

****

After working the photo shoot in LA, Kylie flew to New Orleans so she could be with Fabian. He had a performance at the Superdome, and then he had to do a couple of radio interviews. While Kylie sat in bed completing some work on her laptop, Fabian took a shower. She never told Fabian about her encounter with Fancy nor did she tell him about the deal Fancy did with Gregg. She thought it would be pointless to tell him since he had gotten rid of Fancy. Plus, she knew that it would only make him want to confront Fancy, and Kylie wanted him to have absolutely no further interactions with that bitch.

Fabian came out with a towel wrapped around his waist. He had a nice body, from his tattooed biceps down to his ripped abs. Water beads ran down his smooth skin, which caused Kylie to feel moist between her legs.

"What you lookin' at, girl?" Fabian asked while brushing his hair.

Kylie rolled her eyes playfully. "Not you."

"Yeah right. You know you can't resist me," Fabian said cockily.

"Full of yourself, aren't you?"

"Nah, not really," Fabian said as he climbed under the covers while turning on the TV.

Kylie turned to him. "You wanna see the pictures from my jewelry party?"

"Yeah, let me see them," he said sitting up.

Kylie pulled up all the pictures from her party. While going through them, it put a smile on her face. That was an important milestone in her life, and she couldn't be more blessed. As soon as she came up on the picture of her and Trace, she could sense a little attitude coming from Fabian.

"I see your boyfriend made it," he shot sarcastically.

"Actually, my boyfriend didn't come. He was busy," she retorted.

Fabian shook his head as he continued to look at the picture. "Damn, he got his arm all around your waist and shit. That nigga wants you," he declared.

Kylie sucked her teeth as she got out of the bed. "What about the cover that you just shot with your ex? You guys were awfully cozy," she spat.

"Man, I didn't know they were going to hire her to be the model. That was business."

"Yeah, and I had to find out about it when the entire world did. Why couldn't you mention it before the magazine was released?" she questioned him.

Fabian huffed. "Because that shit wasn't that important. I don't give a fuck about Fancy's ass. It was only business," he stressed.

"Well, this was my business. And Trace does not want me. I told you we're just friends," Kylie said knowing that it was a possibility that Trace had feelings for her.

He cut his eyes at her. "Yeah, well, I don't want you around him. I don't trust him."

"How you don't trust him but you had a number one hit that features him a while back? Where is this coming from?"

'I'm a man, and I know when another man is trying to get at my woman. Trace likes you, and I'm not about to just settle for that 'we're just friends' bullshit. I don't want you around him, Ky."

Kylie shot him a dirty look, not liking his demands. "You are being ridiculous right now. I really can't believe you're making me choose," she said stunned.

"If I'm your man, then that really shouldn't be a hard decision."

"Right now, I don't know who you are," Kylie snapped putting on her shoes.

Fabian had pissed her off to the max and she couldn't believe he had put her in this situation.

"Where you going?" he asked.

"Away from your ass," she snapped as she gathered her suitcase.

"Oh, just like that? So your ass can't take the heat? You gotta run since you didn't get your way?" he asked watching her walk out.

"Yep. Deuce's."

Kylie carried all of her belongings and slammed the door. She walked down to the front desk and paid for her own room. Kylie didn't feel the need to leave the hotel since she would be leaving the next day. Kylie grabbed the key from the receptionist and walked to her room. She turned on the TV and got comfortable in the bed. She replayed the conversation between her and Fabian over and over in her head.

She grabbed her phone and dialed Kellan's number.

"What it do, Ky?" she answered.

"Nothing much. What are you up too?"

Kellan sighed. "I'm handling the work that you didn't finish. Duh," she shot.

"That's what you get paid for. I called to talk to you. Why did me and Fabian get into it?"

"Again? Y'all stay beefin'. What happened this time?"

Kylie relayed the entire argument to Kellan, hoping that she would side with her. She tried to understand Fabian's reasoning, but she wasn't going for it.

"Is he serious?" Kellan asked

"That's what I said."

"Girl, I don't know. When a man starts acting insecure that means he's doing something on the side. You better watch his fine ass," Kellan warned.

Kylie perched her lips. "Nah, I don't think Fabian would cheat on me," she spoke sounding confident.

"Okay, I'm just saying; watch him. And, no, I would not end your friendship with Trace. Trace has been there for you since day one. Why would you give that up?"

"I know. Well, I won't keep you. I'll call you later."

****

On the upper level of the hotel Fabian lay on his back with his hands locked behind his head. His infidelity was making him think irrationally. He didn't mean for the argument to get out of control, but everything had happened so fast. Although he suspected that Trace had feelings for Kylie, he didn't mean to snap at her like that. Every time he was in Kylie's presence, Fabian would have flashbacks of Fancy giving him head. He knew that if Kylie ever found out about their act that she would leave him. The fear of being without her almost made his anxiety rise to an unfamiliar level.

Damn, I'm trippin' from this shit. He declared that day that he would never ever cheat on Kylie again, especially with Fancy.

CHAPTER 19

"Tell me why the hell you left that photo shoot!" Gregg barked in Fancy's face.

Fancy rolled her eyes. "Why don't you ask your receptionist?" she shot.

"What?"

"I said ask that bitch you got working for you! She's running around telling all of my fucking personal business to the whole world! Is that how you run your business?! Do you let your staff go around gossiping about our affairs!" she yelled.

Gregg glared at her. "Are you questioning me?"

"Who, what, when, where, why, how? Do the math," Fancy snapped, then crossed her arms under her breast.

Before Fancy knew it, Gregg had punched her in the face. This time, Fancy fought back with a knee to his groin area. Gregg doubled over in pain while Fancy elbowed him in his back, sending him to the ground. Thoughts of Fabian leaving her and her current state of her life caused Fancy to lash out at Gregg. She repeatedly kicked him all over, feeling the rage rise up inside of her.

Gregg recovered quickly. He caught her foot, which sent her flying backward to the floor, and got on top of her.

"You think you bad, huh?" Gregg yelled in her face

Fancy clawed his face. "Get the fuck off of me!"

"I'm about to give you a thorough ass whooping." Gregg snatched out an extension cord located by his T.V while still holding Fancy down. He pulled out his gun that he always kept tucked on his back and aimed it at her face.

"Strip, bitch!" he demanded as he stood up.

Fancy stood with fear ripping through her body. She began to plead and cry while stripping out of her clothing. She stood naked praying that he wouldn't rape her. Gregg then proceeded to whoop her with the extension cord, striking her all over her body. Fancy's cries became more violent and louder as she pleaded for the beating to stop. Gregg showed no mercy as he swung wildly, tearing Fancy's skin apart. He made sure not to strike her face since she was technically his model.

After about fifteen minutes of a nonstop beating, Gregg finally stopped, leaving Fancy on the floor to cry silently.

"Go get cleaned up so you can give daddy his fix."

★★★★

Kylie sat in her car, contemplating if she should call Fabian. She hadn't spoken to him since their argument, which was a week ago. It seemed like whenever they would be at a good place in their relationship, something would pop off and create a negative situation. Kylie wanted so desperately to call and inform him of some news she had been keeping from him, but decided against it.

Why should I call his ass? He's the one that pissed me off. He didn't call me, so I'm guessing he doesn't wanna talk.

Kylie got out of the car and went inside of her building. She unlocked the door and was greeted with a twenty-six-inch flat screen T.V with a sign on it that read, *"Play me."*

Kylie grabbed the remote and pressed play. Fabian's face popped up smiling while sitting on her bed. Instantly, her heart melted from stubbornness to butter.

"What's up, Ky? I heard that your man is out of town until tomorrow morning. So that leaves us a little time to do what we gotta do. Now I won't tell if you don't, aight? If you down to let me blow your back out, follow the rose petals."

Kylie got excited at the little game Fabian was playing. She followed the petals all the way to her bathroom where the door was closed. She slowly opened the door. Kylie found Fabian sitting on the ledge of her Jacuzzi tub smiling.

"I see you down for whatever," he said while licking his lips.

"I am. You better make sure this is worth my while since my man hates sharing," she spoke seductively.

"Oh, it will be. Come up out of those clothes for me."

Kylie did as she was told and stood in front of Fabian ass naked. Immediately, his dick stood at attention as he eyed her beautiful body. He grabbed her hand, then helped her get into the bath water. The water was nice and hot just how she liked it.

Fabian gave her a glass of wine to help her relax, but she opted not to drink it. She felt so special once again. She loved it when Fabian would cater to her. Most times, he made her feel like she was the only woman in the world.

Fabian grabbed a tray of chocolate cover strawberries which was one of her favorites.

"Thanks, babe. You can be sweet at times," Kylie joked

He laughed. "That's cold, baby."

"I'm just playing."

"I actually want to get some things off of my chest. Is that cool with you?" he asked.

"Sure."

Fabian had thought all day long if he should come clean about his act with Fancy. He was ready to take his relationship to the next level with Kylie, but he didn't want any secrets between them. Earlier, he had made the decision that he wanted to be honest with her. But seeing her face and how happy she was at the present moment made him change his mind. Fabian couldn't bring himself to hurt Kylie, so he opted not to say anything.

"I just wanna let you know that I love you. I apologize for snappin' on you about that Trace shit. I was trippin' like a mothafucka. I still don't like y'all friendship, but I'ma be cool about the shit until I see something I don't like. Besides Kenyon, you're the best thing that has happened to me. I know we've only been together a little under a year, but I can't see my days without you so…" Fabian pulled out a jewelry box and revealed a ten-carat round cut diamond ring.

Kylie covered her mouth as she tried to process what Fabian just subliminally asked her.

"Stop playin', Fabian," Kylie said with a tear rolling down her cheek.

"I'm dead ass, Ky. I want you to be my wife."

"Oh my God. Yes, I will marry you," she said, feeling like her heart would burst from the excitement.

They kissed briefly before Kylie could get a good look at her ring. The diamond was flawless and it looked damn good on her hand.

"Is this from my jewelry line?" she asked.

"Hell yeah. I couldn't go spend my money with no one else when my girl got her own shit. Plus, I didn't want to hear your mouth," he joked.."

"You damn right. You bet' not buy shit from no other company. I can't believe I'm wearing my own line!" Kylie yelled.

Fabian laughed at her theatrics and shook his head. Kylie could be so over the top at times.

"Well, there's something I want to tell you as well," she said staring into his eyes.

"What?"

Kylie sighed slowly. "You're going to be a daddy again."

"Yeah right. Are you serious?"

"Yeah. I found out a while ago. I just wanted to wait until the three-month mark," she cheesed.

Fabian grinned as he thought about Kylie carrying his child. "That shit crack. I can't wait to tell my mama."

"Later for all that. Get in this tub with me so I can give you some of this pregnant cat."

"Shit, you ain't said nothing," Fabian said undressing.

For the remainder of the night, the couple made love as if it would be the last time. Their intimacy level was exalted as they took time with each other's body. Kylie had never been on a natural high like this. She had finally found the man of her dreams who would soon be her husband and the father of her child.

CHAPTER 20

Kellan sat in her bed eating some Ben and Jerry's ice cream. She was enjoying her night off by catching up on *Love and Hip Hop.* While shouting at the TV, her cell phone rang. She looked at the caller ID and was surprised to see that it was Braylon calling. Her first thought was to send him to the voicemail, but then again she did want to hear what he had to say.

"Hello."

"Helen Kellan, what it do?" he asked sounding chipper.

"Nothing," she responded sounding dry.

"I ain't talked to you in a minute. What's been up with you?" he asked oblivious to her tone.

"Working. You know how it is."

"Hell yeah. What you doin' tonight? You should come to The Comfort Zone and have a drink with me," he suggested.

"I'll pass."

"Why not, girl? Come fuck with your boy."

"Hell nah. I'm sure you have someone else who can keep you company. Call one of your other hoes," Kellan snapped.

"I see you on that bullshit. Why you being so mean?"

"Fuck you Braylon, and stop calling me."

"So you really not gon' come out with me?" Braylon asked in disbelief.

"Nope, not interested. I have to go."

Kellan had hung up on Braylon feeling satisfied. He had a lot of nerve calling her when she had caught him with another chick. No, they weren't a couple, but Braylon had expressed to her before that he wanted to see where their relationship could go. Kellan was tired of falling for the wrong guy. She wanted someone who could hold her down through any storm, and Braylon had proven that he wasn't cut for the job.

****

Ever since Kylie had revealed to Fabian that she was pregnant, he had been catering to her every need. When he went out of town, he would call her all day. If she needed something, he would have his mother bring it to her. Kylie loved the attention and was hoping that this feeling would last during her entire pregnancy.

Kylie had made the decision to let Kellan manage the styling business so she could focus more on her jewelry line. Kylie was well aware of the decision she had made, but she didn't want to overwork herself. Although Kylie had made a good living from being a stylist, she now felt that it was time to begin a new chapter. No, she wasn't giving up being a stylist completely; she just wanted to get some other things accomplished.

Fabian and Kylie never had another conversation about her and Trace's friendship, so she still talked with him often. She just couldn't see herself not talking to Trace. Once she told Trace about her engagement and pregnancy, he seemed to be extremely supportive. That was one of the things she admired about him; he was always compassionate.

Kylie walked into Fabian's house ready for a nice bath. Fabian was gone for the next couple of days so she would be all alone. Even though Fabian's house was huge, it still had a cozy feel to it. She went to the kitchen to get a bottle of water. While taking a sip, her phone rang.

"Hello."

"Hi, Kylie," Kenyon said.

"Hey, handsome. What are you doing?"

"Um nothing. Are you at my dad's house?"

"Yeah, I'm here. What's up?"

"Can I come over for the night? My mom is going out and she told me to call and ask you," he said sweetly.

"You sure can come over. You and I can hang out for the night."

"Okay, I'll be there in a little while."

"Okay. Call me when you get outside."

"Bye."

Kylie hung up and smiled to herself. Kenyon was such a well behaved little boy so she never minded when he came to stay with her. She quickly ran some bath water and took a bath before Kenyon came. While trying to relax, she heard her phone going off in the bedroom. She quickly jumped out of the tub and hurried to get the phone, thinking it may be Kenyon. But it was Fabian.

"Hi, honey."

"What's up, baby? Why you ain't answer the phone? I just called you."

"I was in the tub. How was your performance?" she asked

"It was good. Drake came and performed with me."

"Oh, really? I bet the crowd was trippin' out."

Fabian chuckled. "Hell yeah, and it was stupid packed. I'm sleepy as hell after that performance."

"I know you are. Kenyon is coming over to spend the night. So I'm gonna hang with him for the night."

"Word? How is my baby doing?"

"Good. No morning sickness today. Thank God."

"It'll get better hopefully. Well, I'm about to go to sleep. I'll call you in the morning. Send me a pic of them titties while you're at it."

Kylie laughed. "I got you. Bye, baby," she said, then hung up.

After snapping a few pictures for Fabian, Kylie put on her pajamas. The doorbell rang, and she hurried down the stairs to open the door for Kenyon. He stood there with his book bag on his shoulder.

"What's up, man?" Kylie greeted him.

"What's up?" he replied as he came inside.

After waving at Ava, Kylie locked the door. She and Kenyon retreated to the bedroom where he changed into his PJ's.

"Kylie, you know my birthday is coming up?" he told her as he got in the bed.

"Yes, your dad told me. What do you want?"

He thought for a moment as if it was a hard question.

"Um, I don't know because my dad gets me everything I want," he laughed.

"Your daddy has spoiled you."

Kenyon turned to look at her. "So, you're having a baby? Why your stomach not big?" he questioned.

"Because I'm in the early stages. Don't worry; in a couple months my stomach will be huge."

"I'm happy I get to be a big brother. I hope you have a boy," he beamed.

"Why? What's wrong with a girl?"

Kenyon gave her a funny face. "I can't play rough with a girl."

She laughed. "Oh, that's why. You are too funny."

They talked a little more before Kenyon snuggled up with Kylie in Fabian's bed and fell asleep. Kenyon was so happy that his dad had finally dumped Fancy. He would have never come over by himself to be with her. He just didn't like her, but Kylie was different. He could tell that she liked him and that made him happy.

CHAPTER 21

"Hello."

"Fabe, it's me Fancy."

Fabian rolled his eyes. He usually didn't answer unknown numbers but he thought that maybe it was one of his business associates. Fancy had been calling him nonstop since their photo shoot, and quite frankly he was tired of her blowing up his phone. Changing his number wasn't an option so he figured he'd warn Fancy to stop calling him.

"What's up?" he asked dryly.

"I wanna see you. Are you still in New York?" she asked.

"Yeah, but I'm not really trying to see you though."

She smacked her lips. "Why not?"

"'Cause I'm with Kylie, and honestly, I'm not trying to go there with you no more. She's about to have my baby and we're getting married soon. So it's best for us not to talk with each other anymore."

"What the fuck? So you're going to marry her?! What about me, Fabian? I still love you!" Fancy barked, feeling as though her heart would literally break.

Fabian huffed. "Man, I don't want to hear that shit. It's been over between me and you. Stop all of this dramatic shit, for real,"

"What hotel are you at? I wanna talk to you in person," Fancy asked, ignoring his last remark.

"Nah, you don't need to. I gotta go."

Fabian had hung up on Fancy. She couldn't believe what he had just revealed to her. 'Cause I don't fuck with you like that no more and plus I'm with someone else.' She couldn't get that part out of her head. Fancy had calculated in her mind that she and Fabian was just on a break. She just knew that Fabian would come running back to her after she gave him some head in his trailer. Crushed wasn't the word to describe Fancy's feelings. She was hurt beyond anything.

Feeling as though she had to see him, she shot up and began to get dressed. Fancy still knew Fabian and the only hotel that he stayed in when he was in New York was the Four Points, so she made her way towards the hotel. She had met Fabian there on several occasions, but she didn't have a clue as to how she would get in his room.

Fancy hailed a cab and gave the driver the address. When she arrived, she began to concoct a story as to why she needed access to his room. Fancy knew if they called up to his room to say that she was downstairs he would never come down. So it was mandatory that she get a key to his room.

Fancy walked in, then went up to the desk. One of the young ladies who Fancy had seen on a previous night was working.

"Hello. How are you?" the girl asked, recognizing Fancy from the urban blogs.

Fancy put on her fake smile. "I'm good. How about yourself?"

"I'm doing well. What can I do for you?"

"I'm here to see my boyfriend, Fabian, the rapper." Then Fancy batted her falsies.

"Oh, I thought you two had broken up?" the woman asked.

Fancy exhaled before replying. "Girl, you know you can't believe every damn thing. Fabian and I are very much in love and still together," she lied.

"Well, that's good to know. Normally I would have to call him and get permission, but since I know you're his girlfriend, I'll just give it to you," the lady said and handed Fancy the key to his room.

"Oh, thank you," Fancy said with a smile. "I appreciate it."

Fancy swiftly grabbed the key from her hand and jetted to the elevators. She couldn't contain her excitement as she thought, *That was easy!*

After a two-minute ride, Fancy got off, then walked down the hallway to his room. She slid the card in, then quietly opened the door.

"*Fabiaaan*," she sang as she tiptoed in.

She didn't hear a reply so she walked towards the bedroom. She quietly opened the bedroom door and found Fabian snoring loudly. She shook her head and then chuckled. Fancy was tempted to slap Fabian out of his sleep, but she had a better plan in mind. Fancy began to undress, making sure to take off every article of clothing. She grabbed one of the hotel robes and put one on. Fabian was a hard sleeper so she wasn't worried about him waking up. She grabbed his phone and unlocked it. After scrolling to her wanted contact, Fancy went to work.

****

Kylie and Kellan were doing some evening shopping at the mall. They were in Macy's where Kellan was trying on different shoes. While Kylie sat watching Kellan, her phone signaled she had a direct message on Instagram. She opened the message and saw that it was sent from Fabian's account. She pressed play and was very puzzled when Fancy popped on her screen standing in the same room as Fabian. In the background, she could see that Fabian was sleep on the bed. *What the fuck?!*

"Hi, Kylie," Fancy spoke in a low tone. "I bet you didn't expect to see me here with your fiancé. As you can see, I knocked his ass out with this good pussy. Like I told you before, Fabian will always be mine. You thought because he proposed to you and that you're having that bastard child that he would leave me alone? Let me put you up on game, bitch; that will *never* happen. I have to go now, and snuggle up with our man. Oh, and ask ya man what happened at the Rolling Stone's photo shoot. Bye, hoe."

As soon as the message ended, Kylie played it again just to make sure that she wasn't hallucinating. After the second time, she knew that it was indeed a real message.

"This can't be. I gotta be dreaming," Kylie told herself.

Kellan noticed a change in her demeanor. "Ky, what's wrong?"

Kylie continued to shake her head as if the video would disappear. She was desperately trying to will herself not to cry, but she couldn't help it. She gave her phone to Kellan and told her to play the video. Kellan watched the video with her mouth wide open the entire time. She couldn't believe what she was seeing with her own eyes.

After the video was done, Kellan looked at Kylie, who had her hands over her face.

"Ky, are you okay?" she asked her.

"I am, absolutely speechless. I gotta get out of here," Kylie said and got up from her seat.

Kellan hurried and caught up with Kylie, who was walking a mile a minute, but Kellan honestly didn't know what to say to comfort her cousin. When they finally reached the car, Kylie finally broke down.

"It's okay, Kylie. Let it all out," Kellan said as she hugged her.

"No, it's not okay! This mothafucka just proposed to me and got me pregnant!" Kylie yelled visibly hurt.

"I know, honey," Kellan comforted her.

Kylie continued to cry, feeling like her world had been shattered. She really didn't see this coming. She had trusted Fabian and never thought that he may have been unfaithful. Now she was back to square one but this time with little a one on the way.

CHAPTER 22

Fabian woke up feeling refreshed and ready to go home. He had the next couple of days off and he planned to spend it with Kenyon and Kylie. He felt truly blessed that he found someone that completed him. Every day Fabian would wake up with a smile on his face because he knew he had someone beautiful waiting at home for him.

Fabian hopped on the jet and made his way back to Milwaukee. While going through his phone, he noticed that Kylie hadn't texted him like she usually would, but he did see that Fancy had called him. Fabian was really regretting his decision to let her give him some head because she was starting to behave more like a stalker. It seemed as though she always knew what city he was in, which scared him.

After his flight, his car service picked him up and drove him home. While in the car, he called Kenyon and talked to him for a while. When he arrived home, he noticed Kylie's truck parked in the driveway, which got him excited. Sticking his key in the door, he unlocked it and dropped his bags by in the foyer.

Kylie was seated in the kitchen with her back toward the window. She had been waiting for hours for Fabian to finally come home. She had gotten all of her tears out of her system, and now she was ready to snap.

Fabian had finally come into the kitchen with a smile spread across his handsome face.

"What up, babe?" he kissed her on the cheek then took a seat.

Kylie sat there staring at him silently. All night she had been replaying the video, and it caused more rage to rise up inside of her.

"What's up? You sick?" he asked

Kylie rolled her eyes. "No, I'm not sick," she spat.

Fabian gave her a weird look. "Damn, what the fuck is wrong with you?"

"Here, baby; I want you to watch something," Kylie said taking out her phone.

She went to the video and gave it to him while instructing him to press play. She watched intently as his facial expressions changed. Just hearing Fancy's voice made Kylie want to slap all of Fabian's teeth out. When he was done watching the video, Fabian shook his head in disbelief.

"Aye, babe, it's not what you think," he insisted frantically.

"Oh yeah? Enlighten me," she challenged him.

"Um... Shit, I don't know how she got in my room, but..."

Kylie put her hand up to stop him. "I don't want to hear it," she snapped.

Fabian kneeled down in front of her. "Kylie, you gotta believe me. This shit was a setup," he pleaded.

Kylie stood up and began to pace back and forth. "Fabian, cut the bullshit! Your ass got caught!" she yelled.

"This is bullshit, Ky! This bitch set me up," he seethed.

Kylie got into his face not liking the explanations he was giving. "How the fuck did she set you up when she's in your hotel room while you're lying in the bed? Please tell me that."

Sweat beads began to form on Fabian's forehead. He was so frustrated because he was actually telling Kylie the truth. "I don't know how she got in my room. I promise you; when I went to sleep there wasn't nobody in my room."

"I'm not trying to hear that shit, Fabian," Kylie dismissed him.

Suddenly Fabian became furious because she wasn't trying to hear him out. "So you not gon' listen to what I'm trying to say?!" Fabian barked.

"Hell fucking no! I trusted your ass and now look how you do me! I'm sitting here being faithful to your sneaky ass while you're around here fucking with your ex-bitch! The same bitch that was trying to sell your ass to Stacks on Decks Records! I really can't believe you!" Kylie screamed with tears streaming down her face.

"What the hell are you talking about?" Fabian asked, not understanding what she had revealed.

"Oh yeah, that bitch made a deal with Gregg the CEO and promised him that you would sign with them. Now her dumb ass is working off the money that she took. But this is what you wanted, right?" Kylie yelled and then mushed his face.

"Aye, chill out, for real," he warned her.

Kylie stood face-to-face with him and looked him square in the eyes. "Can you honestly look me in my face and tell me you haven't cheated on me with Fancy?" All this time, she had chosen to ignore that remark that Fancy made about asking Fabian about the Rolling Stone shoot. She figured Fancy was just being a spiteful bitch and didn't even feel the need to entertain the thought.

Now, she wasn't so sure.

Fabian looked her in the eyes and tried to form the lie that was so desperately trying to come out, but he couldn't lie to her anymore. The act between him and Fancy had been eating away at him. He was tired of hiding his infidelity from Kylie. It was time that the truth came to the surface.

"Listen; it only happened once," Fabian revealed above a whisper.

Kylie's mouth slightly dropped as her eyes held the pain that was bound to pour out at any second. She could feel her heart literally tearing into tiny pieces.

"You fucking cheated on me with that bitch!" she shouted as she swung and hit Fabian.

Fabian restrained Kylie and pinned her arms behind her back. "Chill the fuck out. Did you forget you're pregnant?" he fussed.

"Fuck you!" Kylie yelled as her tears painted her face.

"It was only once, Ky."

"I don't care! I'm done! Don't call me any fucking more," Kylie snapped and snatched her arms out of his grasp as she stormed out the kitchen.

Fabian didn't even run after her. Minutes later, he heard the front door slam.

"Fuck!" he yelled while punching a hole through the wall.

Fabian's mood had gone from happy to defeated all within five minutes. Fear set inside of his body with the thought of Kylie leaving him for good. Fabian wasn't ready to even think about his life without her. Then his thoughts went to that sneaky bitch, Fancy. She was determined to ruin his relationship from the start.

I'm about to fuck that bitch up!

****

As soon as Kylie arrived home, she went to pack her bags. She had to get as far away from Fabian as possible. The pain that lay within her heart was almost unbearable. The love of her life had committed the ultimate betrayal. Kylie just knew Fabian was it for her. He was the one she wanted to share her life with. But his infidelity kept battering her mind, causing the pain in her heart to expand and take over.

After packing her bags, Kylie ran across a picture of her and Fabian. Looking at the picture made her sick to her stomach.

While I'm being truthful to him, he's still fucking his ex bitch!

Rage returned to Kylie's body, causing her to shoot the picture across the room. Pieces of glass shattered across the floor. Kylie felt some satisfaction from that and then grabbed her cell. She called the only person who could truly help her during this time.

"What's up, Kylie?"

"Trace, I need to come to see you."

CHAPTER 23

Fancy looked down at the mirror, feeling worthless as she stared at the white lines that lay across. She was terribly depressed and didn't know how much longer she could survive like this. Fancy's life had spiraled out of control, and she had no way of stopping it. She didn't have any family support that she could rely on. She had been on her own since she was fourteen, when her mother went to prison for killing her husband. She thought she would feel better once she sent the video to Kylie, but she didn't. Fabian had already called threatening her and refusing to rekindle their relationship when she had the nerve to ask. In her world, she knew Fabian would come crawling back to her, but she was sadly mistaken.

Marsha Ambrosius' *Chasing Clouds* played softly in the background while her tears continued to pour down her cheeks. If she could do it all over again, Fancy would have been a better woman for Fabian. She realized that she had been the problem all along, but she wasn't ready to take it as a loss. To her, nothing was worth living for in her life. Fancy was literally at her breaking point.

Gregg still treated her as his puppet and his personal piece of ass. Her only escape was this white powder that stared her in the face. It took Fancy to a place where she had no cares or worries. She wasn't reminded of the numerous amounts of losses that she continued to cause. With one sniff, Fancy was taken to a place of ecstasy, where she could function without breaking down and crying.

The ringing of her phone snapped her out of her place of elation. She looked at the caller ID and huffed. Gregg had been blowing up her phone for the past hour and a half. She had no desire to talk to him so she pressed the ignore button and snapped back into her trance.

I can't deal with him right now!

****

Kylie stepped off the plane feeling worse than she had been before. Trace had booked her flight to New York after hearing how upset she was. Sitting for two hours really made her think about her current situation. Kylie had always wanted to be married when she finally started having kids, but she was faced with the harsh reality that she could possibly be a single mother. She actually felt sorry for her unborn child because he or she would have to be raised in two different households. Kylie thought about Fabian's indiscretion, and she honestly couldn't see herself taking him back after what he had done.

Kylie walked over to baggage claim to retrieve her luggage. As she was walking, she noticed Trace's driver standing by the door. He came and grabbed her bags from her, and they walked out to the car. She hopped in the back of the truck where Trace was talking on the phone. He patted the spot next to him. After hanging up from his call, he wrapped his arm around her, pulling Kylie closer.

"What's going on, fat mama, 'cause you poking out," he teased.

Kylie playfully hit him. "Shut up," she chuckled.

"You wanna talk about it?" he asked.

"No, not really. I just wanna eat," she smiled.

"Yo' fat ass," he joked.

Kylie smacked her lips. "Duh. I am pregnant."

"Aight. Whatever you want."

They ended up at The Tribeca Grill, where Kylie stuffed her face until she thought she would burst. She and Trace made small talk while eating. Trace was dying to know what had happened that she had to leave Milwaukee right away. He knew it had something to do with Fabian, but he wasn't sure exactly what had occurred.

"I know you wanna know what happened." Kylie told him, then took a sip of her water.

Trace shrugged. "I'm not going to rush you. You can tell me when you ready."

Kylie released a sigh. "Well, I'll tell you the basics. Fabian cheated with his ex. That pretty much sums it all up."

Trace had a look of disbelief written on his face. He never expected Fabian to cheat on Kylie because she was such a good woman. He often wondered how things would be if Kylie was a permanent fixture in his life. He had wanted her since the day they had met, but he never wanted to destroy their friendship. However, now that Fabian had messed up, Trace was more than willing to pick up where he left off.

"What about the baby?" he asked.

"I'm still going to be a mother. Hopefully he'll play his role as a dad," Kylie said with a nonchalant tone, but on the inside it killed her to say that.

Trace nodded his head. "Well, as always, I'm here for you. Whatever you need, I got you. So, since you're here, I'm about to go to the UK and I could use your assistance in the styling department. The stylists I have now be tryin' to have me in some bullshit. I need you like yesterday," Trace said with laughter.

"Of course I will. How can I say no?" Kylie happily agreed.

Trace felt a sense of satisfaction because Kylie would be traveling with him. He always enjoyed her company and loved being in her presence. What the future held for them no one knew, but he prayed that it worked in his favor.

CHAPTER 24

It had been weeks since Fabian had last seen Kylie. He missed her terribly and couldn't get over the fact that they weren't together anymore. Fabian would either call or text day and night, but he was always greeted with her voicemail or no reply to his messages. Without Kylie, his days were longer and were accompanied with remorse. He couldn't eat, sleep, or function without her. If he could turn back the hands of time, he would have done things a different way. Not only was Fabian concerned with Kylie, but he was also concerned about his unborn child. He prayed that she didn't act on her emotions and do something drastic, like get an abortion. That would hurt his heart to the core.

Fabian sat backstage at his concert feeling like a zombie. It felt like he was floating through his days barely getting by. Most days, he didn't want to perform or even get in the studio.

Braylon came in and saw his brother lying on a couch with his hat over his face. Braylon shook his head, feeling like he was failing his brother. He had tried all sorts of thing to get Fabian out of his funk, but nothing he did helped. It hurt him to see his brother in this lovesick phase.

"Bro, you gotta get ready. You'll be going on next," Braylon said tapping him on the shoulder.

"Aight, man."

"You still ain't talked to her?" Braylon asked referring to Kylie.

Fabian shook his head. "Nah, I don't know if she's safe or how the baby's doing. I don't know shit," he spat.

"Don't worry, bro; she'll call soon."

Fabian didn't respond and silently prayed that Braylon was right. He should have thought about the consequences of his actions. Being caught up in temptation had caused him to lose his focus on what was important in his life. The ringing of his phone caused him to snap out of his reverie.

"Who is this?" he answered, not recognizing the number.

"Hey, honey. You finally answered your phone for me," Fancy purred into the phone.

"Bitch, what the fuck you want? You got a lot of nerve calling me when you fucked up my relationship," Fabian seethed with anger.

"I have something that belongs to you. I want you to come get it," Fancy said lustfully.

"I'm not fuckin' with you. I might beat your ass if I see you for real," he threatened.

"So you don't want your precious and expensive dog tag with Kenyon's face on it?" Fancy asked.

Fabian realized that he hadn't seen his necklace in a while, but figured he'd left it somewhere in his bedroom. He would've never guessed that Fancy was the person who had it. His hatred for Fancy had multiplied because her actions to trap him were sickening.

"Send it in the mail," he ordered her.

"Oh, no, honey. I want you to come get this personally. I know you're performing tonight, so I'll send you a text with an address of where to come."

"Bitch, keep that shit. I'm not fucking with your rat ass," he spat and hung up.

Seconds later, Fancy sent a picture with one of Fabian's credit cards in her hand. *What the fuck?* Fabian knew right then that Fancy had stolen his card when she sent that stupid ass video to Kylie. He never checked his wallet when he stayed at hotels and didn't think that Fancy would have the balls to take his possessions.

"What did she want?" Braylon asked immediately.

Fabian huffed. "She got my fuckin' necklace and credit card. I hate this bitch right now," he sighed.

"How didn't you know that she had your card?"

"Because that shit just sits in my wallet. I barely use that one," Fabian explained.

Braylon waved his hand dismissively. "Man, fuck that necklace and you can always cancel that card. Don't give her more ammo to keep fucking up your life," Braylon advised.

Fabian shook his head and went against his better judgment. "Nah, I got some shit to say to this hoe ass bitch. Plus, I wanna whoop her ass for all of this shit she's been pulling."

"Fabian, leave that bitch alone. You have more to lose than she does, and if you keep playing her little games, some shit might pop off for real," Braylon warned.

"Ain't nothing gon' pop off with Fancy soft ass."

"Aight, but I'ma come with you just to make sure," Braylon suggested.

"Yeah, do that. But let me get on this stage."

After giving what was left of his mind, body and soul into his concert, Fabian hurried and changed clothes so he could go meet Fancy. She had texted him and told him to meet her at the hotel where she was staying. Fabian tried to keep a cool head on the way over, but when he thought about the stunt she had pulled, he still wanted to knock her ass out.

"You want me to go in with you?" Braylon asked as they pulled up to the hotel parking lot and parked.

"Nah, this should be quick. I'll be right back."

Fabian got out and walked inside. He called Fancy to come down but she insisted on him coming up to her room instead. He wasn't trying to play into her kid games, but he wanted his belongings. He cursed his way to the elevators. He rode the elevator with an instant attitude. Once he got off the elevator, he walked down the hall to her room. Before he could knock on Fancy's door, she opened the door in some La Perla lingerie and a matching silk black robe.

"Baby, you don't look too happy to see me," she purred with a smirk.

He made sure the door was closed before he backhanded her. She fell onto the bed as she rubbed her face to soothe the burning sensation. She could feel her body shake as she looked into his cold eyes. Fabian had never laid a finger on her during their relationship, so she was scared to death.

He stood there ready to give her more but she remained quiet.

"Now where is my shit? I'm tired of playing this little kiddie ass game with your ratchet ass," he barked

Tears began to pour from Fancy's eyes. "Why don't you love me?!" she yelled.

"Aye, I'm not trying to hear that shit! Just give me my gotdamn shit!" he shouted with a look of fury in his eyes.

"I love you more than that bitch! Why can't you see that? I'm the one you're supposed to marry," she cried.

Fabian looked into her eyes and noticed that they were blood shot red. To him, it looked as though she was under the influence of something. Her skin looked flushed and her pupils were dilated.

As Fabian ransacked the hotel room in search for his things, Fancy continued crying louder as the pain multiplied. She wanted Fabian's heart more than anything, and for him to shit on her made it worse.

"Where is my shit?!" he yelled with this insane look on his face.

Fancy shook her head in disbelief. She couldn't believe that their relationship had come to this. "I tried everything, but you just don't love me like you love her! I need you Fabian!"

Fabian pointed to her face. "Aye, you're fuckin' insane. Do you know that you ignorant ass bitch?"

"I'll show you insane. How about I call your bitch and tell her that I'm pregnant," she spat, while grabbing her phone and searching for Kylie's number, which she had stolen out of Fabian's phone that night at the hotel. Once Fancy saw her name, she pressed send and listened as it began to ring. Fabian instantly smacked the phone out of her hand where it landed across the room.

"Have you lost your fuckin' mind? Why are you so obsessed with me?"

"Because we're soul mates! If you don't wanna be with me, I promise I'm going to kill myself," she threatened.

"Do that shit!" he scoffed. "I'm about to leave," he said without thinking twice.

"Fair enough; you win. If I can't have you, then I don't wanna live. My death will be on your hands, Fabian!" she shouted.

She walked over to the balcony and opened the doors. She walked out and gripped the railing. Fabian looked back at her shaking his head. He couldn't believe the behavior that she was displaying.

"Aye, what the fuck are you doing, Fancy?" he said watching her stand on the balcony.

She ignored him while she prepared for her suicide. Fancy was done with life. She had no more fight left in her. Waking up every day had been such a struggle for her, and she welcomed her fate with open arms.

Fabian didn't believe her dramatics, so proceeded to walk toward the door. That's when he heard the railing break. When he looked back and no longer saw Fancy standing there, he immediately ran to the balcony.

"Fancy!" he yelled.

Fabian looked down and saw Fancy's body splattered on the ground thirty-two stories below. He stood there paralyzed in complete shock. He didn't want to believe that Fancy had actually jumped to her death. *Fuck, fuck, fuck!* he gritted to himself. Fabian was praying for Fancy to be okay, but he knew deep down that there was no way she had survived that fall. Fabian could see pedestrians rush over to her body. He pulled out his cell phone, called 911, and then rushed down to the lobby. Instead of taking the elevator, he took the stairs feeling as though the elevator would take too long. His heart felt like it would explode from the sudden adrenaline rush. Fabian prayed that this was somehow a dream that he would wake from at any minute.

When he got downstairs, he ran outside and towards the crowd that was gathered around her body. Braylon had gotten out of the truck to see what the big fuss was. When he saw who it was, he gasped.

"Bro, what the fuck happened?" he asked Fabian in a panic tone.

"She jumped from the balcony. This shit is fuckin' crazy," Fabian exclaimed, running his hands down his face.

Minutes later, an ambulance pulled up. From what Fabian could see, Fancy appeared as if she had no more life in her. When a white sheet was placed over her body, Fabian began to pace back and forth. Braylon came over to him and tried to calm him down.

"You gotta tell me what the fuck happened up there," Braylon insisted.

Fabian planted his hands on his head. "We started arguing, and then she said she was about to kill herself and her ass jumped. I can't believe this shit!"

Soon after, police cars filled up the parking lot. One detective came over to Fabian asking him a series of questions. He tried to answer them to the best of his ability but was still in shock. He couldn't understand what would possess Fancy to commit suicide.

"Sir, we're gonna have you come down to the station for further questioning," the detective stated.

Fabian obliged and hopped in the police car, instructing Braylon to trail them down to the police station. He sat in the back of the car traumatized by the sight of Fancy's lifeless body. A feeling of remorse came over him because he had told her to do it. Never in a million years would he think that Fancy would have actually jumped off of a balcony. If his life wasn't in shambles an hour ago, it was definitely fucked up now.

CHAPTER 25

"So, can you tell me how you ended up at the hotel?" Detective Cowan asked Fabian.

Fabian released a sigh. "I told you, she had a piece of my jewelry and my credit card, so I went to go get it after my show," he said for the fourth time.

"Okay, so you went to get it and what happened from there?"

"When I got there, we started to argue. She told me if I didn't want to be with her, she would kill herself and went on the balcony. I didn't believe her, so I went to leave. Then I heard the railing break on the balcony. I ran to the balcony and saw that she.... had jumped." It pained Fabian to repeat that part of the story.

"So why was the hotel room in shambles?" the detective asked with a raised brow.

Fabian huffed in frustration. "Because I was trying to look for my stuff. She wouldn't give it to me. That's how she operated. She played a lot of fucking games."

"Explain to me why there was a bruise on the victim's right cheek?" the detective asked.

Fuck! Fabian thought to himself. He had forgotten all about the slap that he had delivered to Fancy. *Damn, should I tell the truth or what? This mothafucka looking at me like I killed her ass.*

"I don't know," Fabian lied.

"I think you do know. You were the last person to see her before her death. A lot of things are not adding up to me."

Fabian gave him a screw face. "What the hell you tryin' to say? You think I had something to do with her death?" Fabian asked incredulously.

The detective stood and began to pace around the room slowly. "You go see her to get a so-called necklace and credit card, which wasn't found in the room by the way. Then she has a bruise on her cheek, you don't know how it got there, and now you're saying she jumped to her death. This sounds like bullshit," Detective Cowan barked.

"I didn't do shit to her! I'm telling you the truth! What the fuck I gotta lie for?" Fabian yelled.

"What do you have to lie for?" the detective mocked. "You're one of the top selling rappers in the industry. You have several endorsement deals. Your album has sold over a million records and your career has skyrocketed to the top. So, yeah, you have a lot to lose, but truth be told, you're going to jail for murder, Mr. Fabian Bryant."

"I'm not trying to hear that shit. Get my lawyer in here," Fabian spat.

"Smart move," the detective said as he left out of the interrogation room.

Everything was at stake; his career, endorsements and freedom. Then he suddenly thought about Kenyon and his unborn child. At the thought of his kids seeing him in jail, especially for a crime he did not commit, his panic began to thunderously multiple.

****

Kylie stood in front of a floor length mirror inspecting her now round belly. She had a cute pouch that could easily be hidden with a blazer or jacket. At four months, she wondered how big her stomach would get. Last night she had finally felt the baby move, which made her more excited to be a mom. If only she could have shared her excitement with Fabian, it would have made it much more special. She still hadn't talked to him, and she honestly didn't want to. Kylie was still hurt by his infidelity and most of all she had lost trust in him.

Being on the other side of the world hadn't been much of a vacation for Kylie. Trace had tried his best to cheer Kylie up. She appreciated his attempts to the fullest, but she couldn't help but think of Fabian. Lately, Trace had been becoming more of a flirt than anything. He was always throwing out remarks about them being together. Kylie tried to ignore it, but Trace just wouldn't let up. Why couldn't they just remain friends? Her mother had told her a while ago that men and women couldn't succeed as being friends, and Kylie was starting to believe it. There was no doubt that she loved Trace, but her love for him was only platonic.

"What's up?" Trace asked, startling her.

Kylie covered her chest with her hand. "Damn, you ever heard of knocking?" she snapped.

"Damn, my bad. Why are you snappin'?"

Kylie caught herself and took a deep breath. "I'm sorry. What's up?" she asked in a softer tone.

"Tonight I'm going to the premiere of the movie *Fifty Shades of Black*. I was wondering if you wanted to be my date."

"No thank you. I'll pass. I don't want people getting the wrong impression."

Trace twisted his face into an irritated scowl. "Fuck what people gotta say. I want you to come with me," he said walking up on her.

"I can't. I'd rather play it safe. I wouldn't want anything getting back to Fabian or his people."

Trace sucked his teeth. "Why the fuck are you still hung up over him?" he snapped with a hint of jealousy.

"Because he is still the father of my child. And I'm not hung up over him, so stay the fuck out of my business, okay?" Kylie snapped, knowing damn well she thought of Fabian night and day.

"Oh, so now I gotta stay out of your business? Aight, you got that," he said, then walked out of the suite.

This mothafucka is really dancing on my nerves!

The more time she spent with Trace, the further he pushed her away. He was starting to have too much nerve commenting on her relationship with Fabian. Yes, it was her that shared her heartbreak with him, but she didn't expect him to throw it in her face. Kylie decided after this week that she was heading back to the states so she wouldn't have to deal with him.

CHAPTER 26

"It's official. They're charging you with second-degree murder."

"Get the fuck outta here! I didn't kill that bitch!" Fabian roared at his attorney.

Braylon had called Fabian's lawyer right away, and he'd met them at the police station.

"I know you didn't kill her, but you know how the MPD can be. They're not going to do a thorough investigation if they have who they think the suspect is in their faces," his attorney informed him.

"What evidence do they have to charge me with this bullshit?"

His attorney sighed and loosened his tie. "Well, your fingerprints are on everything inside of the room. The victim apparently had a bruise on her face. They went through her cell phone and found old angry messages from you in which you threatened bodily harm. Also, the receptionist told them that you went to the hotel room in a rage. There's enough probable cause to issue an arrest warrant. It does look bad, but I'm going to do everything to get you out."

"Well, did they see my fingerprints on the balcony?! If they don't have my prints on the balcony that means they ain't got shit on me!" Fabian barked with rage visible in his eyes.

The lawyer touched his shoulder in an attempt to calm Fabian down. "Don't worry; I'm on top of that. In the meantime, I'm going to work with your brother and publicist so we can do damage control. The media is going to have a frenzy with this story."

Fabian sunk in his chair feeling all kinds of emotions.

Why me? he kept saying to himself. He regretted going over to her hotel room. Braylon had warned him not to and now he wished he would've listened to him. A part of him was saddened by the fact that Fancy committed suicide. He never wanted to see her die, even after all the hell she had caused in his life. But now his life and career were on the line, and he couldn't afford to lose anything. Fabian was now in the fight of his life.

It was time to prove his innocence.

****

Kylie began to pack her bags for her departure to the states. She hadn't told Trace that she was leaving; he would know once he noticed that she wasn't there anymore. She missed her home terribly and was ready to get back to her own work. Kylie's days of mourning her relationship were now over. It was time to look out for herself and for her child.

As Kylie packed her last bag, her cell phone rang.

"Hello," she answered.

"Ky, I have some dirt for yoooou," Kellan sang.

"What?"

"So I get a call from Vogue Magazine and they wanted to know if it was possible you could style their next shoot for double of what they would originally pay you. I asked why they were doubling the fee. Get this; Trace is telling everybody that you're his personal stylist and there's no way he would allow you to work with anyone else."

Kylie gasped. "You're lying!"

"I'm so serious, and this is not the first time I've heard this. Trace is definitely blocking you from working with other people, and I wanna know what his problem is, shit," Kellan snapped.

Kylie huffed at the news Kellan had just told her. "Like for real, this dude is really pissin' me off. Since when did he become my manager? You know, the last couple of weeks he has really been irritating me. I'm about to curse his ass out before I hop on this plane. I'll call you when I touch down."

"Aight. Handle your business," Kellan said and hung up.

Kylie hurried and dialed Trace's number. He had told her earlier that he was going to his sound check. She waited impatiently as his phone rang and rang. After about five rings, his phone went to voicemail. Kylie was going to leave a voicemail but quickly decided against it.

I'm not about to waste my time with his ass! He'll catch my drift when I'm gone with the wind.

****

Fabian was finally booked at district one police station in downtown Milwaukee. He was taken to the booking department where his mug shot was taken, along with his fingerprints. The officer read to him the official charges that were being brought on him and then Fabian changed into the jail uniform.

Fabian's attorney came to speak with him once again, letting him know that there would be a court date for the following day. His attorney also said that he was hoping that the judge would give him a bail so he wouldn't have to fight the charge in jail. Fabian prayed like never before hoping that he would get a bail. After meeting with his lawyer, he got a chance get to a phone call. He decided to call his mother.

****

Monet had just gotten off the phone with Braylon, who gave her the news about Fabian. She wanted to break down and cry because she knew her son was innocent. After talking to Braylon, she decided to call Fabian's lawyer so he could give her the details on the case. The entire family had gathered at Monet's house when they learned of Fabian's arrest. Everyone knew Fabian was innocent; it was just a matter of proving it. As everyone sat around in deep thought, the house phone rang.

"Hello," Monet answered.

"You have a collect call from ...*Fabian*... Do you accept the charges?" the automated system asked.

"Yes, I accept... Fabian?"

"What's up, mama?" he replied sadly.

"Oh my God, son! What the hell is going on?" she asked almost crying.

"Man, they trying to say that I killed Fancy. Mama, you know I didn't do this, right?"

Monet nodded her head. "Of course I do. I've been praying that they find some kind of evidence that says otherwise. I just found out that you go to court tomorrow. We'll all be there," she assured him.

"Thanks, but do me a favor; don't bring Kenyon. I don't want him to be around all this."

"Okay. I'll let Ava know. You still haven't talked to Kylie?"

"Nah, but I gotta go. I love you, and I'll see you tomorrow."

"I love you too, baby."

CHAPTER 27

Kellan sat in her car waiting for Kylie to emerge from the airport. She hadn't seen Kylie in a couple weeks so she was excited to see her. While waiting, she listened to the Breakfast Club show. She always got a kick of out of Charlemagne's donkey of the day. As they were talking, Kellan heard them mention Fabian's name, so she turned up the volume.

"We have breaking news. Multi-platinum rapper, Fabian, has just been charged with the murder of his ex-girlfriend, model Fancy Nicholson. Reports say that the incident happened on Wednesday night. More to come on this story."

Kellan covered her mouth with her hand in total shock. She couldn't believe what she had just heard. She wondered if Kylie had heard of the news. Kellan thought about calling Braylon to get some details but quickly decided against it since she hadn't been speaking to him on a regular basis.

Kylie finally came out with her luggage in tow. Kellan popped the trunk for her, then waited anxiously for her to get inside of the car.

"What's up, cousin?" Kylie said with glee.

Oh Lord. She doesn't know, Kellan thought. "I have some news for you," she said slowly.

"Oh God. What now?" Kylie said scrolling through her phone.

"Fabian's in jail," Kellan blurted out.

Kylie immediately turned to look at her with a puzzled face. "Why?"

"They say for killing Fancy," Kellan winced.

Kylie's mouth dropped open. She was hoping that this was a joke. She was waiting for Kellan to say something like "I'm just playing," but she didn't. Kylie knew Kellan was telling the truth because she had a serious look on her face.

"Wait. Hold up... Did you really say for killing Fancy?"

Kellan nodded. "Yeah, that's what the Breakfast Club just said."

"So, she's dead?" Kylie asked again trying to tie everything together.

"Um yeah. Killing means dead."

Kylie sunk back in her seat and tried to process what was just revealed to her. She knew something had to be wrong with the situation. The Fabian she knew would never lay a finger on anybody, let alone kill someone.

Did Fancy drive him to that point? Would he really kill her over breaking us up?

Her thoughts suddenly went to her child. Was she really ready to raise a child on her own? God forbid if Fabian had to do some serious time behind this, because she didn't know if she would be able to handle being a single parent for a long period of time.

When Kylie got home, she hurried and turned on the TV, searching for some kind of story on Fabian. When she didn't see anything, she hurried and took out her laptop. She went straight on TMZ and saw that it was the first story. She read the entire article feeling like everything was a nightmare in the making. Critics had painted Fabian to be this cruel and dangerous man, when really it was the opposite. Kylie instantly felt sorry for Fabian. She couldn't imagine what he was going through. She wanted to reach out but the reports had stated that he hadn't posted bail yet so she decided to wait.

****

Fabian entered the courtroom on pins and needles. He had prayed all night that the judge would grant him a bail. When he walked in, he saw his entire family seated, including Ava. A part of him wished that Kylie would've showed up, but he knew deep down that she still wasn't fucking with him. His attorney was sitting next to him gathering his paperwork together. When the judge came in, everyone stood.

"The state vs. Fabian Bryant with the charges of second-degree murder. How does the defendant plead?" he asked.

"Not guilty, your honor," Fabian's attorney stated.

"The next court date is set on March 26th. What's the matter on bail?"

"Your honor, I don't think bail would be a good idea for the defendant. He has the means to flee the country," the district attorney argued.

"Excuse me, your honor, my client has obligations he needs to fulfill such as his tour dates and promotional appearances. On top of that, he has a son to take care of, so fleeing the country wouldn't be feasible," Fabian's attorney countered.

The judge sat for a moment before he replied, "Bail is set at one million dollars, in which I order the defendant to house arrest until further notice. Court is adjourned," the judge announced, banging his gavel before leaving the courtroom.

Fabian sighed with relief. He wasn't excited about the house arrest, but it was better than fighting this case behind bars.

****

Fabian was released hours after his court hearing. He ended up posting his bail with cash. Immediately after being released, he was sent over to an agency that specialized in house arrest. From there, Fabian verified his address along with his phone number and case number. After all of his referrals were received. He was then given his black ankle bracelet that would have to accompany him everywhere. Fabian chuckled sarcastically a bit because he had never pictured himself in this position.

Since he was coming home, Monet had prepared a nice hearty meal just to relieve a speck of his stress. Fabian was always on the go 24/7, and now he had to be in the house all day and night. Braylon had to cancel his hectic schedule, along with a bunch of other important priorities. His publicist was working hard to control all of the negative press, but it was getting way out of hand. Every single day there was a story or article regarding Fabian's charges. He was also advised to stay off of any social networks, such as Facebook or Instagram. Fabian had come to the terms that he was living under a microscope now and that it was going to be an uphill battle from this point on.

He arrived at his house feeling uneasy. His entire day had been surreal to him. Fabian questioned his ability to prove his innocence. While he knew he was not guilty of murdering Fancy, the doubt remained in his mind if the jury would know as well.

He walked into his living room where his family was seated watching TV.

"What's up y'all?" he said flopping down in his seat.

"Are you hungry? I made some dinner," Monet told him.

"Nah, my appetite is gone."

Everyone looked away feeling empathy. Fabian looked defeated and that broke everyone's heart because he had always been the strong one in the family. Kenyon walked in and saw that his dad was finally home. He had wanted to see him for days, but Ava would always tell him that he was out of town.

"Dad!" Kenyon ran with glee.

Fabian's face had lit up as well because he too had missed his son awfully. Seeing Kenyon's face was actually like a breath of fresh air.

"What's up, man? I missed you," Fabian hugged him.

"I've been waiting for you to get home. Dad, where's Kylie? I haven't seen her in a while."

Kenyon's question had caught him off guard. He tried to block Kylie out of his mind but found it hard to. He also understood that Kenyon and Kylie were close, so it had to be strange for him not to see her anymore.

"Kylie has been working, man," Fabian lied.

"Okay. Can I stay here with you, dad? Please?"

"Yeah, man, whatever you want," Fabian smiled, kissing him on the cheek.

CHAPTER 28

"I am a little concerned about your weight. You should have gained more weight than eleven pounds," Kylie's OB-GYN, Dr. Sensei, expressed to her.

Kylie sighed. "I've been very stressed lately. Most days I don't have an appetite," she revealed.

"Well, you know the baby comes first. You have to eat regularly; three meals a day with snacks in between."

Kylie nodded because she knew what her doctor was saying was very true. Everything was hitting her all at once. Thinking about Fabian's possible murder charge had her on the edge; also being pregnant and lonely was starting to take a toll on her emotionally. Kylie wanted to talk to someone about it but didn't know who. Of course she had Kellan, but at times, she was sure that Kellan was tired of hearing about her problems.

"I need a referral to see a therapist. Do you think you can help me with that?" Kylie asked her.

"Definitely. If there's any way I can help, then I'm all for it. What I do recommend is for you to get some rest. Traveling back and forth across the country is not good for your body, especially when you're carrying a little one. Okay, Kylie?" she smiled.

"Yes, I hear you."

"I'll get that referral for you right away," Dr. Sensei said before leaving out of the room.

Kylie sat and thought for a few moments. Her body was definitely tired, but she had work to do. She didn't want to sit at home and think about her depressing situation.

Lord, there has gotta be better days ahead, Kylie prayed.

****

Fabian sat in his home studio writing new material. It had been a month since he had begun his house arrest and it was driving him crazy. He needed something to take his mind off of his current situation, so he decided to let his music do the talking. Just as he was about to get inside of the booth in his at-home-studio, Braylon came in.

"What's up with you?" Fabian greeted him.

"Man, I just got off the phone with a representative from Sprite. They dropped you."

Fabian shrugged. "I was expecting that. Not really shocked at all," he said as if he wasn't fazed by it.

"Man, I tried to convince them, but they weren't having it. The good thing is Adidas hasn't called. I think they might still rock with you," Braylon assured him.

"Oh yeah? I hope so," Fabian said shaking his head.

"I do have some good news though. You were nominated for a BET award," he smiled.

"I would be happy if I was able to attend the mothafuckin' award show," Fabian chuckled with Braylon laughing out loud.

"You a fool, bro. You still ain't heard from Kylie?"

Fabian shook his head. "Hell nah. Her ass ain't tried to call to see if I'm okay or anything. I told Tre to ride by her house, but he didn't get an answer when he rang the doorbell. I shouldn't have to reach out to her when I'm the mothafucka who's on house arrest. Regardless of how our relationship ended, I still expected to hear from her. I mean, she's carrying my child, and I don't know shit about the progress of her pregnancy or nothing. So fuck her," he vented.

"Shit, I feel you on that. I hope she don't act like this when the baby is born. And I hope she don't try to keep you away from your child."

Fabian cut his eyes at Braylon. "She knows not to ever play with me like that. We'll really have a problem if she tries that bullshit."

"Do you even know what y'all havin'?"

"Nope. I'm sure it will be a boy, though. You know we don't produce girls," Fabian chuckled.

"You don't know that shit."

Interrupting their conversation was the doorbell. Fabian walked to the front door where he was greeted with Kenyon and Ava.

"Hey, dad," Kenyon said walking in.

"What's up, man?"

"Hey, I figured I would bring you something to eat," Ava said holding up some carryout containers.

"Thanks, Ava," he said stepping to the side to let her in.

Lately, Ava had been very supportive of Fabian. She was calling all the time to check on him and would stop by with food. Fabian appreciated her kindness and wasn't surprised by it at all. Even when they were together, Ava was always thoughtful. Fabian was glad that he still had a good relationship with her because most men couldn't stand their child's mother.

"So I see you still have fans," Ava smiled after they all gathered in the kitchen to eat.

Fabian stuffed some food into his mouth. "What do you mean?"

"People are still showing you love on Twitter and Instagram. I think you have more followers too."

"I love my fans. They're loyal as fuck."

"So what's up with the case?" Ava asked.

"I'll tell you later," he said signaling that Kenyon was still in the room.

Suddenly, Braylon rushed into the kitchen and said, "Aye, turn to TMZ."

Fabian grabbed the remote and turned on the TV in the kitchen. When he turned the channel, there was a story about Fancy's suicide.

"*The coroner's office has received the toxicology reports back on Fancy Nicholson and those reports show that there was an excessive amount of cocaine in her system along with the drugs ecstasy and OxyContin. This could have possibly played a role in her death, but officials are not releasing any statements at this time. More to come on this story.*"

Fabian turned the TV off and looked at Braylon. He was hoping that the toxicology reports would help prove his innocence. Fabian was a little shocked because he had never known Fancy to do any kind of drugs. The most he had ever seen her do was drink.

"Maybe this will help your case," Braylon spoke.

"I hope so cause I'm losing money," Fabian said.

****

Kylie and Kellan were at Pro Nails located on Milwaukee's north side getting their monthly pedicures. Kylie was in total bliss as the technician scrubbed her swollen feet. She still had been working but not as much as she normally would. Thoughts of Fabian still crept inside of her mind causing her to miss him more. But being with him would probably hurt beyond anything, so she chose to stay away. Snapping her out of her reverie was Kellan's voice.

"Ky? Did you hear me?" she asked.

"What?"

"Girl, they found all kinds of drugs in Fancy's body. She was high as hell."

Kylie shook her head. "Word?" she asked shocked.

"Yep. Have you talked to Fabian?"

"No."

Kellan turned to look at Kylie. "Why not?"

"Because I'm not ready to talk to him yet. I'm still hurt," Kylie said sadly.

Kellan smacked her lips. "Damn, Kylie, you ain't even tried to call his ass? Girl, you better put your feelings to the side and at least show him that you care. I mean, damn, this man is facing a murder charge, who happens to be the father of your child. Why would you just shit on him like that?" Kellan shot.

"I know it sounds bad, but..."

"But nothing. You're being selfish, Kylie. Overall, Fabian was good to you, despite his infidelity. Just call him to show that you care. Have you even told him the sex of the baby?" Kellan inquired.

"No, I haven't told him anything," Kylie said, sounding almost ashamed of her actions.

Kellan chuckled. "Girl, you'll be lucky if he don't put the goons out on your ass because you need your ass beat. You are acting real ratchet. As a matter of fact, don't be claiming me as a family member either."

"I am not acting ratchet," Kylie snapped.

"Yes, you are, and as your family, I'm here to tell you the truth. Call the man at least."

"I'll think about it," she said, just as her cell phone rang.

She looked at the caller Id and was surprised to see that it was Trace calling. It had been weeks since she had left him in London and now here he was calling her for the second time.

"Hello."

"What's up, Kylie? I've been calling you. What's going on?"

"Nothing. Just working," she answered dryly.

"Oh word? How's the pregnancy going?"

Kylie sighed because she could tell that he was trying to feel her out. "Straight. Why did you tell everyone that I was your stylist? I mean, you blocked a lot of people from booking me," she said, cutting straight to the chase.

"I only told my manager that, and when I said it, I meant it as a joke. I didn't think he would go running his mouth."

Kylie smacked her lips. "Yeah, tell me anything," she said as if she didn't believe him.

"I'm serious. Do you really think I would stop your hustle? Think about it."

"I don't know. I'll think about it."

"You do that. Aye, but I got a show in the Mil tonight and wanted to know if you wanted to come. You can bring whoever you want."

Kylie thought for a moment on if she wanted to be in Trace's presence. He seemed like he was telling her the truth so she let go of her attitude towards him. "Oh wow. Maybe I'll step out tonight. I'll see if Kellan wants to go. I'll call you later, okay?"

"Aight. Be easy," he replied and then hung up.

Kylie hung up the phone, then looked over at Kellan. "That was Trace. He claimed he only said that statement as a joke."

"I'm sure," Kellan smirked.

"Oh and he has a show here tonight. You down?"

"You know it."

"Now I gotta find something that looks good with this belly."

CHAPTER 29

It was overly packed at the US Cellular Arena for Trace's concert. Since Kellan was coming, Kylie made sure to invite her other girls since everything was on Trace. So Kylie made her way through the crowd with Kellan, Ana and Calise. Dressed casually chic and comfortable, Kylie sported jean jacket with the sleeves cut out and a white wife beater with some black leggings. Since her ankles were swollen, she scratched the heels and sported some combat boots. Her hair was in a bone straight wrap with her makeup done to perfection. To be six months pregnant Kylie still turned heads.

After a short wait, the opening act for Trace graced the stage, who happened to be singer Kehlani. She rocked the crowd with her certified hit "The Way". After she had done her thing, Trace came out blazing the stage with hit after hit. Kylie looked on in awe because Trace was an amazing performer. The way he kept the crowd hyped up was amazing.

After his show, Kylie and the girls traveled backstage to speak to Trace. When they came into his dressing room, he was guzzling down a bottle of water. Once he saw Kylie, a smile lit up across his face. She still possessed that baby glow that he had admired.

"What's up y'all? What's up with you, Miss Kylie? You look nice," he greeted them.

"Thank you and great show. I almost forgot how good you were," she teased him.

Trace laughed. "Don't even play me like that," he said, giving her a hug.

Meanwhile, the girls were posing for pictures and the photographer kept snapping. Kellan loved the camera and would never pass up a moment to pose.

"So what's new? You should be ready to pop soon."

"Yes. I got about twelve more weeks," she said anxiously.

"What are you having?"

"It's a secret," Kylie smiled.

"Oh, it's like that? I can't know?" he smiled flirtatiously.

"No, sir. Fabian doesn't even know yet. But that's here nor there," she said with a wave of her hand.

"Are you having a baby shower or what?"

Kylie shook her head. "I am not in the mood to have one. I told my aunt and Kellan not to give me one. I've still been buying everything though."

"Well, anything else you may need, let me know. I'm here until Friday."

"Sounds cool. So what are we about to get into?"

"Y'all hungry?" he asked

"I thought you would never ask."

****

Fabian sat in his home office feeling bored to death. The house arrest was starting to take a toll on him mentally. He was basically in prison but within his own home. Even with his family and friends stopping by on a daily basis, it still wasn't enough. He missed the rush of his old life, where flying from coast to coast was a weekly ritual. Fabian missed going to events where flashing lights were an initiation of the celebrity scene. Most of all, he missed the high of being on stage. There was nothing like performing in front of thousands of fans who adored him. Thinking about all of it made Fabian angry all over again.

Turning on his laptop, Fabian began to search the internet. He was tempted to log onto Twitter but decided against it. He didn't want anything jeopardizing his case, so he remained disciplined when it came to that. Deciding he wanted to catch up on the entertainment world, he browsed the celebrity blogs. One title in particular caught his eye, which read *"Which rapper is the daddy? Trace or Fabian?"* So he clicked on it. What he saw was something that almost made him puke. There were numerous pictures of Trace and Kylie hugged up, along with pictures of Kellan. Fabian could feel his rage rise up inside of his chest as he counted to ten. His feelings were incredibly hurt while he looked at the two.

This bitch got the audacity to be hugged up with this man while I'm here suffering! he ranted to himself. *She ain't not once called to see how I'm doing or how my case is going. I really can't believe this bitch. Prancing around the city pregnant with my baby. I could slap her ass for real.*

It was moments like this where he would rush to the studio, but he was too pissed to rap about anything. He hurried, shut his laptop and went downstairs. No words could describe the pain that stung his heart. The love of his life had betrayed him in a way he never thought would happen. Even through the fire, Fabian always thought Kylie would be there for him, but it was evident that she couldn't care less. With the way his life was going, he was aching to shed a tear, but his pride wouldn't let him do it. Instead, he poured himself a glass of Patron and let the alcohol take him to another place. His first trial date would be coming up, which happened to be on his birthday, and Fabian desperately needed to get his mind off of Kylie so he could focus.

****

After Kylie and her crew had accompanied Trace and his entourage out to eat, she opted not to go out. She thought it was a little tacky to be pregnant and at the club. While everyone made their way to the party, she carried herself home. Once she got inside, she jumped in the shower and threw on her pajamas.

She laid down with the thought of Fabian on her mind. She thought about what Kellan was saying earlier about her reaching out to him. After going back and forth inside of her mind, she grabbed her phone and reluctantly dialed his number. Before it could ring, she instantly hung up.

Damn, why am I so nervous?

Mustering up her courage once again, she dialed his number. This time, she let it ring. As it rang, her heart was almost in her throat as her nervous jitters increased. After three rings, she finally heard the voice she had been yearning to hear for months.

"Hello."

"Hey," she said almost above a whisper.

"What's up?" he asked dryly.

"I was just calling to see how you were doing."

"I'm good," Fabian replied with a roll his eyes.

"How is the case going?"

"Fuck all that. You know what Kylie? I would appreciate if we only talked about the baby. We don't need to talk about shit else," he shot bluntly.

"Okay. Why are you being so rude?" Kylie asked, taken aback by his attitude.

Fabian sucked his teeth. "You're really going to ask me that shit when I haven't heard from you in months? Then you have the nerve to be hugged up with that bitch ass nigga, Trace, while you're carrying my child. Kylie, you're a fucked up person. You really have some fuckin' nerves."

"You know what? I was trying to be nice and call to check on you but fuck you! You're not my fucking man anymore," she hissed.

"I can tell by your actions that it was *fuck me*. And another thing, because I'm on house arrest and can't go with you to the doctor, please call and update me about my child, aight?"

"Well, damn. Whatever the hell you want," she shot sarcastically.

"Bye."

Kylie looked at the phone in astonishment. Fabian had really blew her off, which made her feel more stupid for reaching out to him. She couldn't help but let the tears roll down her cheeks as she thought about the coldness in Fabian's voice. She tried to understand his anger and hated the way he'd just spoken to her. Kylie refused to stoop down to his level and play tit for tat. If he wanted to act like an ass toward her, then he would have to do so with her not around.

CHAPTER 30

Sitting on the passenger side of the car, Fabian prepared himself for his first trial date. He found this day to be surreal because he never thought he would spend his birthday in court where he was fighting for his freedom On the outside looking in, he appeared to be calm, but on the inside his nerves were shot. He was well aware that this was going to be a battle, but Fabian was determined to prove his innocence.

Pulling up to the courthouse, he saw that his lawyer was talking to reporters. As soon as Braylon let him out, the media swam over to Fabian and began to bombard him with question after question.

"What were Fancy Nicholson's last words? ... Mr. Bryant, are you prepared to do a maximum sentence of life in prison?"

Fabian continued to walk inside, not uttering a single word to anyone. Dressed to the nines in a Tom Ford grey wool suit, along with some black Gucci dress shoes, Fabian still looked scrumptious. He had grown a longer, fuller beard, which added to his sex appeal, and his skin was still flawless as always.

Fabian walked in and noticed his family sitting quietly. He winked at his mom, then took his seat at the defendant's table.

Soon after, the judge came in and took his seat.

The prosecutor stood and then made his opening statement. He made Fabian out to be a low life killer who didn't respect women. He was determined to destroy Fabian's character. The prosecutor even brought up lyrics in his songs that made him out to be a murderer. He made Fancy out to be this beautiful model that was nothing more than a sweet individual with a successful career.

After the prosecutor's statement, Fabian was so angry that was ready to walk out and leave, but his attorney instructed him that it was all a part of the process.

Then Fabian's lawyer proceeded with his opening statement, which he portrayed Fancy out to be this mentally disturbed individual who was obsessed with Fabian. He also boasted about how Fabian was an avid leader in the community that had multiple charities with two of them being in Milwaukee. Fabian thought he had done a great job at representing him. After presenting more statements, the judge set another court date.

Since it was Fabian's birthday everyone was gathering at his house for a get-together. Monet had made this huge dinner along with several desserts. Fabian thanked God for the twenty-eight years He had blessed him with.

When he walked into his house there were balloons and decorations everywhere. His entire family was present, including his entourage and people that worked with him. Even though his day had consisted of being in court, he was still happy to be around his family.

"Bro, you getting old. You like thirty-eight, right?" his brother, Tre, joked.

"Ha! Thirty-eight these nuts in your mouth," Fabian joked grabbing his manhood.

"Hey, stop that talk," Monet scolded him.

"My bad mama," he said as he kissed her on the cheek.

Monet continued to set the table while everyone mingled with each other. Every five minutes, Fabian's phone kept ringing with "Happy Birthday" calls. He was grateful that people still cared for him.

After eating, people broke out the bottles of Patron and Hennessey so they could now really let loose. It felt good hanging with his family and having fun. For a split second, he thought about his last conversation with Kylie and how he'd snapped at her. While he didn't regret it, he still felt a little bad.

Kenyon and Ava had arrived fashionably late. Kenyon ran up to him holding a picture wrapped in gift wrap with a bow.

"Dad, I got a present for you," he said with excitement.

"For real? Let me see what you got."

Fabian took the picture out of his hand, then opened it up. Once he saw what it was, he smiled. It was a drawing of himself and Kenyon. It wasn't a professional drawing but was good enough to frame.

"This shit is hot. Who did this?" he asked.

"I did," Kenyon smiled.

"Man, you did your thing on this. I love it. You got skills," he told him as he kissed Kenyon on his cheek.

"I kinda messed up on your eyes."

Fabian shook his head. "Nah, you did a good job. Where should daddy hang it?" he asked Kenyon.

"Um, how about in your room?"

"Aight, I'ma do that. Thanks, man. Daddy loves you."

"I love you too." Kenyon ran out the room to play with his cousins.

Fabian sat the picture in a safe place, then looked over at Ava. She had recently dyed her hair in some honey blonde streaks. Fabian took notice of it and liked what he saw. He wasn't sure if the alcohol had him thinking that or what. Ava was very nice looking with her caramel colored skin and slanted eyes. She sometimes reminded him of the singer Monica.

"Happy birthday. You're pushing forty, right?" Ava joked.

"Everybody got jokes tonight. Don't get your ass kicked out," he teased.

Ava playfully waved her hand at him. "Oh whatever. You like my hair?" she asked.

"Yeah, it's nice. Who did it?"

"Latrece. You know I'm not letting nobody else touch my hair."

"It looks good on you."

They stared at each other a minute more before Ava walked away.

After hours of nonstop partying, everyone left to go home. The only people that were there were Kenyon and Ava, who had helped him clean up. Fabian was passed tipsy while trying to watch TV. Kenyon was fast asleep on his lap. Ava came in and sat next to him where she tried to watch TV. She too was tipsy from all of the Patron being passed around.

"You drunk?" she asked him.

He looked at her in his lazy grin, then replied, "No."

"You jackin'. You still don't like to admit when you're drunk," she laughed.

"I'm not for real."

He got up and put Kenyon on his shoulder. Fabian then took Kenyon into his bedroom and laid him down. He walked back into the living room and sat back down. Ava looked at him with lust filled within her eyes. It had been years since Ava and Fabian had been intimate, and the alcohol in her system was urging her to explore his body. Yes, it was Ava that had decided to end her relationship with Fabian because she felt like she was more attracted to women. But lately she had been evolving mentally and wanted to try dating a man again. Deep down, Ava wanted a husband to love and take care of her. He returned the same look before they met each other with a kiss. It had been years since they had both shared a kiss and the feeling was good. Fabian softly caressed her breast while she held his face. They were both horny and needed to get one off. Fabian picked Ava up and carried her to his bedroom where they made passionate love all night long.

****

The following morning, Fabian woke up feeling slightly nauseated. He didn't feel good at all. When he turned over to his right he saw a figure with hair. Fabian swiftly sat up, not knowing who the person was. He looked over at the face of the woman and cursed under his breath.

Why is Ava in my bed? He looked under the cover and saw that Ava had on her panties but with no bra. Instantly, Fabian hopped out of bed and grabbed his cell phone. He walked all the way down the stairs to his studio. He dialed Braylon's number and waited for him to answer.

"Yeah?" he answered groggily.

"Bro, guess who's in my bed?" he said frantically.

"Who?"

"Ava."

Braylon laughed hard. "Get the fuck outta here."

"True story. I'm trippin' off of this shit too."

"Damn, did y'all fuck?" he asked.

"Shit, I don't know. I was fucked up last night."

"Oh, you hit that pussy then. Ain't no questions about it," Braylon laughed.

Fabian smacked his lips. "Man, this shit ain't funny. I don't want her getting the wrong idea."

"Y'all might as well get back together and be a family," Braylon laughed some more.

"Fuck your ugly ass. I'm out." Fabian hung up the phone and went upstairs.

He walked to the kitchen where he saw Kenyon stepping on a stool trying to grab some cereal out of the cabinet.

"What you doin', boy?" Fabian asked startling him.

"I'm trying to get some cereal."

"I'll get it. Get down before you hurt yourself."

Fabian grabbed the cereal and made Kenyon, along with himself, some cereal. They both sat down at the table and shared a conversation. He was hoping that Ava wouldn't walk in looking as though she had stayed the night. He cursed himself for backtracking with Ava. Fabian prayed that she wouldn't catch feelings for him because he honestly loved the way things were between them before. Now, he was faced with the possibility that they may have damaged their relationship.

"Dad, when is my baby brother coming?" Kenyon asked smacking on his breakfast.

"It should be soon, maybe in another month or two. How you know it's a boy?" Fabian quizzed.

"Because Nana told me."

"When did she tell you this?"

"A long time ago. She said it's going to be a boy because it's all boys in the family."

Fabian chuckled and shook his head. His mom had no hope of ever having a granddaughter. Thinking about the baby caused him to smile inside. He too wondered how the baby will look or if his and Kylie's genes would mix well. Interrupting his daydream was Ava. She came in fully dressed, which was a good thing.

"Good morning, fellas," she said taking a seat at the table.

"Mama, how did you get in here?" Kenyon asked.

"The door was open already. Why you wanna know nosy?" she said pinching his cheeks.

He smiled. "I was just asking."

Finished with his cereal, Kenyon got up and ran out of the kitchen. Ava looked at Fabian with an awkward smile and shook her head. Fabian was wondering what was going through her head.

"For the record, last night *never* happened," she laughed.

Fabian breathed a sigh of relief and began to chuckle. "Sounds good to me. I was a little worried we may have fucked shit up."

"Nah, we'll just pretend that I went home and you went to bed."

"Cool."

CHAPTER 31

Kylie walked into her office feeling like a zombie. She was almost in her last month of pregnancy, and she couldn't wait to drop this load. Her nights consisted of nothing but tossing and turning. On a good night, she would get *maybe* five hours of sleep. Last night, she had stayed up decorating the baby's room. No one knew it yet, but Kylie had found out that the baby was a girl. She was happy to have her own mini-me. She kept going back and forth in her head on if she would give the baby Fabian's last name. With the way he had treated her last time they talked, she was ready to throw her own last name on the birth certificate.

"Don't we look tired today?" Kellan teased.

Kylie rolled her eyes at her. "Girl, this will be my last child. I'm so serious," she complained.

"Come on. It can't be that bad."

"You try carrying this big ass belly around for nine months. Then you can't sleep because you're uncomfortable or have to pee. I haven't slept on my back in months. My ankles are so swollen, and I got heartburn all day every day," Kylie vented.

"Damn, I take that back. At least you still look pretty."

Kylie rolled her eyes again and logged onto her computer. She checked the sales of her jewelry line, which were doing exceptionally well. Kylie and her team were now working on a new set of designs. While searching in her drawer for a calculator, she spotted her second cell phone.

"Damn, I forgot about this phone. I probably have so many messages."

Kylie powered the phone on and saw that she had twenty-one text messages and fourteen voicemails.

"Kells, don't you wanna go through this phone for me?" Kylie asked sweetly.

"No, ma'am."

"You know what? I'm gonna start paying your ass minimum wage," she threatened.

"And then I'm gonna take my talents elsewhere," Kellan shot.

Kylie ignored her and started going through the messages. Each message was either business related or styling requests. When Kylie got to the last message she couldn't understand what was going on.

What the hell is this?

She replayed it again and couldn't believe her ears.

"Kellan hurry and come listen to this message!"

Kellan came over and grabbed the phone from Kylie. She listened intently to the message. Kellan had a look of shock written on her face as well. What they had just heard was very disturbing.

"What are you gonna do?" Kellan asked her.

"I'm going to take this over to Fabian's so he can hear it."

****

Fabian had been back and forth to court for the last two weeks. The trial would be ending, which made him nervous because his fate would be turned over to the jury. His attorney had worked hard trying to prove his innocence. Everything was looking good for him, but the law wasn't designed to help a black man, so it was a chance he could end up in jail.

As usual, Fabian's house was packed with family and friends. Some days, Fabian enjoyed the company, but then there were times he would rather it be just him and Kenyon. Everyone sat in the den watching the BET awards to see if Fabian would win Best Rap Artist. In the midst of watching a performance, they heard the doorbell.

"Aye, somebody get the door!" Fabian yelled.

Kenyon heard his dad and went to open the door. When he opened it, a smile stretched across his face.

"Kylie!" he yelled with glee.

"Hi, baby. I missed you," she said hugging him tight.

"Where have you been? I haven't seen you in a long time?" he asked.

"I've been working and getting ready for the baby."

"Oh yeah. I can't wait to see my baby brother," he beamed.

"Aww, how sweet. Is your dad here?" she asked.

"Yeah. Come on," He grabbed her hand, then walked her to the den.

Kylie became nervous because she hadn't seen Fabian in months. When she walked in, everyone was surprised to see her; especially Fabian. Instantly the feelings that he tried to bury for her came to the surface. She looked so beautiful, and he kicked himself for missing most of her pregnancy. She had the cutest baby bump. Her skin was glowing, and her hair hung freely down her back. It seemed to him that she had a sparkle in her dark brown eyes that she hadn't possessed before. Kylie was casually cute in a gray long sleeve shirt that hung off her shoulders and hugged her belly. She also wore some black leggings, which had become her best friend, and gray suede Jeffrey Campbell booties.

"Hello, everyone." Kylie greeted, sitting down on the couch.

"Well, what do we owe this pleasure?" Monet asked happy to see her.

"I came to talk to Fabian."

"Damn, you fat as hell now," Braylon joked.

Kylie laughed. "Shut up."

"So how have you been feeling?" Monet asked.

"Tired and ready to give birth."

"I know you are, honey. You're due pretty soon, right?" Monet asked.

Kylie nodded. "Yes, and I can't wait."

"Well, you call me because I wanna be there. Don't play with me, Kylie," Monet warned.

"I won't, I promise." Kylie then diverted her attention to Fabian. "Can I talk to you?"

"Yeah, come on." Fabian got up and Kylie followed him to the kitchen.

They both sat at the breakfast bar and stared deeply into each other's eye. Kylie looked at the person who still had her heart. She missed those kissable lips painting her skin with kisses. Everything about Fabian made her weak, but she couldn't fall victim to his sex appeal because he still couldn't be trusted.

"So what's up?" he asked, playing with his fingers.

"I have something that may help your case."

"Like what?" he quizzed.

"It's a voicemail that was left on my other cell phone. I think it was the night Fancy was killed. I think you should hear it." Kylie took out an envelope that contained a cd and her phone records. Fabian wondered how a voicemail ended up on Kylie's phone. Then he suddenly remembered Fancy calling Kylie to lie about her being pregnant and him smacking the phone out of her hand.

"Damn, thanks," he said praying that it would really clear his name.

"You're welcome."

"How's the baby? Do you know what the sex is?" he asked.

"The baby is good. The organs are developed and everything. No, I don't know the sex. We'll see when the baby comes," she lied with a smile.

Fabian nodded. "Aight, and thanks again for doing this. You don't know how much this means to me."

"I didn't do this for you. I did this for my baby and Kenyon. I don't want them growing up without their dad, and I also believe that you didn't kill her."

"Aight, I can respect that," he chuckled.

She got up and walked out and Fabian followed. She stopped and said bye to the family. Monet made it her duty to remind Kylie to call her when she went into labor. Kenyon came and gave a hug.

"Kylie, why you gotta leave?" he asked.

"Because I'm hungry and sleepy, honey."

"You can eat here. My Nana made some food, then you can go upstairs and lay down," he suggested, which caused Kylie to chuckle. She figured Fabian hadn't told him about their breakup.

"Maybe next time, okay? You know you can call me whenever you want. We can still hang out, okay, handsome?" she assured him, kissing his cheek.

"Okay."

Fabian walked Kylie to the door where he let her out and watched her get in her car. For some odd reason, watching Kylie leave hurt Fabian a little. He'd missed those days where she would spend the night or when he would come home to her waiting for him in his bed. Fabian had been trying to get over her, but she was his true love. He had never felt this kind of love with any other woman.

After walking Kylie out, Fabian went downstairs and played the cd.

"You out of your fuckin mind? Why you so obsessed with me?"

"Because we're soul mates, and if you don't wanna be with me, I'm going to kill myself."

"Do that shit. I'm about to leave."

"Fair enough, you win. If I can't have you, then I don't wanna live. My death will be on your hands, Fabian!"

There was a slight pause and then he heard himself asking, *"Aye, what the fuck are you doing, Fancy?"*

Then there was another long pause before he heard himself yell, *"Fancy!"*

There was another pause before Fabian heard himself call 911. *"Shit, shit, shit! Hello? I have an emergency at the Hilton hotel on Wisconsin Avenue. My ex-girlfriend just jumped off the balcony. Please send an ambulance,"* he said in a frantic tone.

Afterward, Fabian heard a noise that sounded like a door closing. He couldn't believe his luck. He looked at the phone records which showed that this voicemail occurred around the time of her death. He said a quick prayer and dialed his attorney. Fabian immediately told him about the voicemail. After listening to it, his attorney assured Fabian that it would get him off. Since his lawyer was still at his office, he instructed Fabian to have someone bring over the voicemail. Fabian went back upstairs and told everyone about the new evidence. Everyone got anxious, hoping that this would help his case.

"Braylon or Ant, do you think one of y'all could run this to my lawyer's office real fast?" Fabian asked.

"Yeah, I'll do it," Ant offered.

"Please don't lose this. It's too important," Fabian stressed.

"I'll make sure he won't. I'll ride with him," Braylon assured him.

"So is that what Kylie brought over?" Monet asked him.

"Yep."

"That was nice of her. Some chicks wouldn't help out the man who cheated on them," she told him.

"I know. She said she did this for the baby and Kenyon, which I could respect," he said.

"I don't know how you let her go. I could slap you," she scoffed.

"Mama, come on now. I already know I messed up. You don't have to rub it in."

"Yes, I do. Now let me go talk to Jesus about this evidence."

CHAPTER 32

Fabian got dressed to attend his last day of court. On the previous court day, each piece of evidence was presented to the judge and jury. The prosecutor also presented three witnesses to testify, including the receptionist at the hotel, and also the detective and coroner. During the cross-examination, Fabian's attorney tried to shred the detective to pieces. Fabian's attorney thought about putting him on the stand, but he decided against it. He didn't need anything ruining the case and there may have been a possibility the case could go really bad.

This drive to the courthouse was much different from the others. Fabian was over the edge and couldn't settle his mind. His thoughts were all over the place thinking about the case. Not knowing what was to come was like torture for Fabian. It had to be one of the most difficult days of his life. When he arrived, as usual, the media was all over the place. It took him a while to get inside.

Fabian walked to his seat and noticed that Kylie was sitting next to his mom. He couldn't believe she had come to support him. He was ecstatic, but didn't want to show it, so he put his poker face on and sat.

"I filed a motion to dismiss the charges, but the judge didn't think that the voicemail was sufficient evidence to dismiss the charges, so the ball is in the jury's court. But I'm almost certain my closing argument will seal the deal, along with this voicemail," his attorney told him.

Fabian simply nodded his head, then turned his attention to the judge.

After a while of going back and forth between the two attorneys and presenting evidence, it was time to seal the deal.

"Council, you may present your closing argument," the judge said.

The prosecutor stood. "Yes, your honor... I want you all to take a good look at this gentleman here. This is a rapper who belittles women in most of his rap songs. He raps about women in the most disrespectful and impertinent manner I've ever heard. The truth is, Fabian Bryant is a cold blooded killer who has not once showed remorse for his actions. Let's think about the victim here. Fancy Nicholson was in love with this man, who was ultimately the cause of her death. She didn't ask to be killed. All she ever wanted was Fabian Bryant's love. So I'm asking you today to put this man where he needs to be, and that is behind bars. I'm asking that you find him guilty. I rest my case."

As the prosecutor walked back to his seat, Fabian's attorney stood up and took the floor.

"Ladies and gentlemen of the jury, my client is a successful rap artist trying to reach the top. His career is the center of his life. Do you think he would kill someone and jeopardize his successful reputation? He has too much to lose, as in his career, his family and most importantly, his freedom. Let's be real about something, Fancy Nicholson was a deranged woman who was obsessed with my client. She went to extreme measures to get his attention. You all heard so yourselves on the voicemail. She said out of her own mouth that she would kill herself if she couldn't be with Fabian Bryant; not to mention the numerous amounts of drugs that were in her system. When someone is high off of that many narcotics, their behavior and thinking process becomes irrational. I'm asking you all today to let the evidence tell you the truth, which says my client is innocent... No further words, your honor."

Fabian's attorney returned to his seat, feeling like he had delivered the closing statement of the year. The judge then turned everything over to the jury and they went to deliberate. Everyone gathered outside of the courtroom deciding on what to do in the meantime.

"Y'all wanna go eat? It's a restaurant down the street," Braylon suggested.

"I guess man," Fabian said looking for Kylie.

Kylie was coming out of the bathroom when she saw Fabian. He looked to be calm but knowing Fabian, she knew he was extremely nervous.

"You hungry? We're about to go eat," he asked her.

"Sure."

Everyone walked out of the back exit so they could avoid the reporters. While walking, Fabian inhaled the fresh air, praying that this wouldn't be his last day on the streets. Kylie caught him in deep thought, then smiled.

"You nervous?" she asked.

"To be honest, hell yeah," he replied.

"Don't worry. I said a prayer for you. God never disappoints."

Fabian smiled at her. "Thanks for being here. It means a lot."

"Of course. Even though we're not together, I still want us to be cool. We're about to share a child, and I don't want us to be at odds."

"I can do that."

They reached the restaurant where they sat inside. Fabian's nerves were so shot that he couldn't even eat. He had no appetite whatsoever. The only thing he did was sat in silence and stared at the TV by the bar. Ava had sent him a text saying good luck and that she wished she could be there. Lately, Ava had been texting him more than usual. Fabian figured she was just as nervous as he was, thinking he would now be out of Kenyon's life forever.

Kylie glanced at Fabian a few times and felt a little sympathy for him. Overall, Fabian was a great guy and didn't deserve what he was going through. She couldn't imagine the emotions that were moving through him. She had been praying for him because she refused to take her child to a prison to see her father.

Everyone sat at the restaurant while talking and eating. They all were praying for this nightmare to come to a close.

An hour and a half later, Fabian got the call that the jury had reached a verdict.

"Aye, we gotta go. They reached a verdict," Fabian said as he hopped out of his seat.

Everybody jumped up as Fabian made sure to help Kylie out of her seat. They all practically ran back to the courthouse. Fabian met his lawyer in the hallway where they walked in together and sat. Kylie locked hands with Monet and Braylon as they anxiously awaited the verdict.

"Jury, have you reached a verdict?" the judge asked.

A man stood up and faced the judge. "Yes, your honor. In the case of Fabian Bryant, we the jury find the defendant... Not guilty."

The courtroom erupted in a cheer while Fabian instantly sat down in his seat and began to thank God. A huge weight had been lifted off of his shoulders and now he was a free man.

"I told you I would get you off. We did it," his lawyer beamed.

"Thanks, man. I owe you big time," he replied while shaking his hand.

Monet was crying tears of joy as she hugged Kylie. Kylie was super excited as well. Even though Fabian had hurt her deeply, she still loved him immensely. Fabian turned around and walked toward his family hugging everyone. Monet cried in his ear while hugging him tight. She almost made Fabian tear up, but he managed to keep it all in. Then he looked at Kylie and smiled.

"Thanks, Ky. I owe you a lot," he said hugging her and kissing her on the cheek.

"I know," she chuckled.

Everyone walked out on cloud nine. This time Fabian didn't mind facing the reporters. All of them rushed up to him asking question after question.

He simply replied saying, "I told y'all I was innocent."

****

Everyone retreated back to Fabian's house, except for Kylie. She had work to do, so she went to her office. Fabian couldn't believe he was free from all the scrutiny that Fancy's suicide had caused. His trial had been all over the TV and internet, causing all kinds of ruckus. People were tweeting stating that they knew Fabian was innocent.

"Aye, bro, everybody is hitting my line showing love and the talk shows are requesting interviews. You ready to tell your side of the story?" Braylon asked.

"Don't schedule anything until after Kylie has the baby. The first thing I need to do is get in the studio with Tim and get these tracks done," he replied.

"Aight cool."

Fabian sat at his dining room table in deep thought before his mother came over to him.

"Baby, I am so proud of you. Not once did you crack under this extreme pressure. I thank God for saving you from that life sentence, and I also thank God for blessing me with a strong minded son," she told him with tears in her eyes.

"Thanks mama," he replied truly humbled.

CHAPTER 33

A couple days later...

"Hello," Fabian answered groggily.

"Fabian, it's me. My doctor told me to go to the hospital," Kylie told him.

Fabian looked at the clock and saw that it was four o'clock in the morning.

"How long you been having contractions?" he asked.

"All night. This shit hurts," she complained.

"Aight. Um, you want me to come get you?"

"Yeah. Hurry up."

"Aight. I'm on my way."

Fabian hopped up and threw on some clothes. He made sure to brush his teeth and wash his face. Knowing that labor can be a long process, he packed his Macbook and iPad just to keep busy. Fabian made his way to Kylie's house within twenty minutes.

When he knocked on Kylie's door, she answered looking like she had been suffering all night.

"You good?" he asked.

"No. Let's just hurry up," Kylie said as she bent over on the couch.

"Did you pack a bag for the baby?"

"Yeah, it's right there."

Fabian grabbed her bags and helped her down the stairs and into the car. He hurried and made his way to the hospital. He held Kylie's hand the whole way while she continued to have contractions. Once they got to the hospital, they checked Kylie in and put her in a private room. Fabian didn't want anyone interrupting their happy moment. He called his mother to let her know that Kylie was in labor. Kylie had received an IV because she had become so dehydrated. It seemed as though Kylie's contractions had become unbearable. Fabian saw that she was crying silently, so he went over to coach her.

"Just breathe, Kylie."

"I can't. It takes my breath away. Tell the nurse I want an epidural," Kylie demanded.

Fabian called the nurse in and told her what Kylie wanted. The nurse wanted to first check to see how much Kylie had dilated.

"I don't think you'll have time to get an epidural, honey. You're already ten centimeters," she said.

"Damn, that was fast," Fabian joked.

They only had been at the hospital for an hour.

The nurse smiled. "I know right? I'll go get the doctor."

"Damn, girl, you really not playing, are you?" he teased Kylie.

Kylie smiled back through the tears as she anticipated seeing her baby. She managed to text Kellan and told her that she was at the hospital. There was a knock at the door, and then Monet walked in with Adrian and Braylon.

"Hey, honey, how you doin'?" Monet asked Kylie.

"In pain. I'm getting ready to push though."

"Wow, that was fast."

Braylon walked over to Fabian. "You ready to be a daddy again?" he asked.

"Hell yeah. I think I'll be done after this."

Dr. Sensei walked in with her blue scrubs on while she introduced herself to everyone.

"So you're ready to push I hear," she told Kylie.

"Yes. Can we please get started because these contractions ain't no joke," Kylie pleaded.

"Sure thing."

The nurse came in with the surgical technician who began prepping the instruments. Monet, Braylon and Adrian went to the family room. They saw Kellan on the way there. Kellan and Braylon locked eyes for the first time in months. There was an undeniable attraction that even Stevie Wonder could see.

"Hey, how's Ky?" she asked.

"She is getting ready to push now," Monet replied.

"Damn, already? That was fast as hell."

"I know."

Meanwhile in the delivery room, Kylie was preparing to push. Fabian stood on her side holding one of her legs while the nurse held the other one. Kylie prayed once more that she would deliver a healthy baby.

"Okay, Kylie, I need a big push, okay? I know you're in pain, but I need you to put all of your energy into pushing," Dr. Sensei said.

Kylie simply nodded her head and prepared her mind and body to push.

Come on, Kylie. Push this baby out! she told herself.

Kylie began to push as if her life depended on it.

"That's it, Kylie. Keep going. I can see the baby's head."

Kylie continued pushing, and before they knew it, the baby was out, crying and hollering all over the room.

"It's a girl!" the doctor announced.

Fabian couldn't believe what he had heard until the nurse laid the baby on Kylie's stomach. He looked at his daughter in awe as tears gathered in his eyes. She was so beautiful with her jet black curly hair and slanted dark eyes.

"Here you go, dad; cut the umbilical cord," the nurse said giving him a pair of scissors.

Fabian cut the cord, then looked at Kylie, who was crying. She couldn't believe she was now a mommy. She was crying mainly because she wished her mother was around to share this moment with her, but she felt her presence in the room.

"I can't believe you gave me my daughter," Fabian whispered in her ear.

The baby was weighed and cleaned off, then the nurse gave her to Kylie to hold. Once Kylie looked into her slanted eyes, she felt complete. She had never experienced a love like this. She was beautiful beyond her imagination.

"What are we going to ask her?" Fabian asked.

"Yeah, Shai Fiona Monet Bryant," which was both of their mother's names.

"I like that," Fabian agreed.

Fabian walked out to the family room where his other brothers had come out and also Kellan's mother, Fallon. When he walked in, everyone was looking up at him awaiting the news.

"Guess what?"

"What?" they all said in unison.

"It's a girl!"

"Oh my God! Don't play with me, Fabian," Monet threatened him.

"I'm not. Come on."

Everyone hopped up and followed Fabian back to the room. Kylie was still holding the baby when everyone came in. Monet rushed over so she could get a good look at her new granddaughter. She was so happy to finally have a girl in the family.

"My baby is gorgeous, looking like her Nana," Monet boasted.

Kellan stood on the side of Kylie as she snapped pictures. "Ky, she is too cute."

"I can definitely see a little of Fiona in her," Fallon told her, thinking of her sister.

"What's her name?" Braylon asked.

"Shai Fiona Monet Bryant."

"Aww, that's pretty," Monet beamed.

Fabian stood staring at the beautiful creation he had made. She was truly a gift from God. He was grateful for the chance to be here for Kylie. He couldn't imagine not seeing his daughter come into the world. Kylie had passed the baby off to Fabian since he hadn't held her yet. Shai looked right into her daddy's eyes, and at that moment, she had captured his heart. Kellan had snapped a few pictures of Fabian while holding Shai.

"So we finally have a girl in the family," Braylon smirked.

"So it's all boys?" Fallon asked Monet.

"Yes, ma'am. Five sons and five grandsons. So as you can see, I am extremely happy."

"That's funny," Kellan said.

"Maybe when you have your baby, you can give us another girl," Kylie teased.

"Girl, bye. I'm not having any kids," Kellan declared as she rolled her eyes at Braylon.

Kylie laughed and shook her head. "We'll see."

****

Two days later, Kylie and baby Shai were released. Kylie was so glad to be at home where she could eat some real food and not be bothered. Fabian took Shai out of her car seat and went to her room to lay her down. Kylie had decorated Shai's room in a yellow and a peach color scheme. All of her furniture was white. Kylie had even painted her name on the wall. Fabian was impressed, to say the least. He gently laid the baby in her crib, making sure there were no stuffed animals or pillows around. Fabian kissed her on her cheek and then left out of the room.

"Aye, Kylie your ass be lying and shit," Fabian said walking into her room.

"What are you talking about?" she replied lying in her bed.

"I'm assuming you decorated Shai's room before she was born, which tells me you knew what you were having, right?"

"I plead the fifth," she smiled.

"Lying ass lil' girl," Fabian laughed.

"I'm sorry. I just wanted you to be surprised. That's all."

Fabian nodded with a smirk on his face. "Don't even trip. I got you… You gon' be alright here by yourself with the baby for the night?" he asked.

"I should be. I know you're tired so go home."

Fabian smacked his lips. "Come on, now you know I will stay if you need me to. I know you're still sore. I'm used to being tired and not getting any sleep. It's the life of a hustler," he smirked.

"Yeah okay, *hustler.* You can stay, and please go get Kenyon because I miss him and he wants to see his baby sister."

"I know. I'm about to go get him now. I'll be back."

****

Fabian stopped home and took a shower. He was now feeling a sense of peace take over his life. He had cleared his name out of an alleged murder and he now had two beautiful kids. The next thing to do was get back on his music grind, which wouldn't be a problem. Fabian had so many lyrics in his head that he knew when he was done spittin', he would have at least thirty to forty songs. He prayed that the roadblock he had just endured would be his stepping stone to his career.

Fabian also prayed for Fancy's soul. He would never have imagined that she would end up taking her own life. He could only pray that God would have mercy on her soul.

After getting dressed and packing an overnight bag, Fabian made his way to Ava's house. When he arrived, the door was already open, so he let himself in. He found Ava and Kenyon in the kitchen eating.

"Dad," Kenyon said running to him.

"What's up, man?" Fabian said, kissing him on the cheek.

"Hey. How's the baby?" Ava asked.

"She's good. She just came home from the hospital not too long ago."

"Can I go see my sister, please?" Kenyon pleaded.

"Yeah, man. Go pack your bag," Fabian smiled.

Kenyon ran out of the kitchen and to his room to get his bag together. Fabian sat down at the kitchen table while waiting for Kenyon.

"So are you happy you finally have your girl?" Ava asked.

Fabian smiled. "Yeah, she definitely gon' make me soft."

"Aww, that's really sweet. What's her name?" she asked.

"Shai."

"That's cute," Ava said clearing her throat, "Fabian, I wanted to talk to you about something."

Aw shit! What is this about? Fabian thought to himself.

"Like what?" he asked.

"It's about the night of your birthday. I've been thinking about it and... I don't know; it kind of stirred up some feelings that I didn't know I had for you. I know I've been living my life as a lesbian, but I believe it was just a phase. I don't wanna date women anymore. Lately, I've been thinking about what we could've been and what we used to share. What I'm trying to say is that I miss you," she revealed.

Damn, Fabian would have been lying if he said he didn't see this coming, but he did. He didn't mean for any of this to happen, but it did and now it was up to him to choose his words carefully and make it right.

"Ava, you know I love you no matter what, and right now I don't feel like that would be a good move for us because I like the way our relationship is now. I know what happened that night, and to be honest, it shouldn't even have gone down, but it did, and I'm sorry if I led you on. Honestly, I'm in love with someone else, and I'm not trying to hurt you 'cause I care too much about you," he replied.

"Fabian, you don't think about us not even a little? You mean to tell me that night didn't mean anything to you?" she asked hoping he would consider.

"I mean, we were both drunk, so we can't go off of that. You said so yourself that we should pretend like this never happened. Let's just leave shit the way that is."

Ava sulked in her seat. "You still love, Kylie, huh?" she asked.

"Yeah, and that's where my heart is."

Ava looked at Fabian visibly hurt. She wanted things to go back to when they were twenty-one years old, but her selfishness had ruined their relationship. She couldn't blame anyone but herself. Ava thought that being with a woman was what she desired, and back then, she had hurt Fabian with her confession. Now the tables were turned, and she was feeling the pain he had felt years ago.

"Okay, Fabian, I respect your honesty. Congratulations on your new daughter," she said and left the room.

Kenyon had finally come out with his bags ready to go. "I'm ready, dad."

"Aight then. Let's go."

CHAPTER 34

It had been two weeks since Shai was born, and Fabian was still in total bliss. Every day had been spent getting to know his little princess. She was a good baby who rarely cried. Kylie was still trying to adjust to being a mommy. She was used to being on the go and making moves. Now her days consisted of breastfeeding and catering to Shai's every need.

Fabian had been a huge help since day one, but now he had to leave and go work on his album. On the way to the airport, Fabian had stopped by Kylie's before leaving. He hated leaving Shai and wished he could stay, but he had already lost time with his trial, so he needed to get it done.

"Daddy's gon' miss his baby," Fabian cooed while holding her.

Kylie smiled at him while folding some clothes. She too would miss him, but wouldn't dare say it.

"Man, I don't wanna leave her," he told Kylie while kissing Shai's cheeks.

"I know, but you need to get your album done. The fans are waiting," she said hyping him up.

"You're right. Make sure you answer your phone, aight? And later on I wanna Facetime you," Fabian instructed her.

"Yes, father," she joked.

Fabian gave Shai one more kiss before laying her in the bassinet. He looked over at Kylie and smiled on the inside.

"You gon' be okay by yourself for two weeks?"

Kylie looked up at him. "Yeah. I'm a pro at this shit," she joked.

"Yeah right. Your ass probably gon' be calling me tonight crying and shit," he laughed. "But for real, if you need any help, my mama is only one call away. I thought about hiring a nanny for you, but I really don't want a stranger around my baby."

Kylie nodded her head, agreeing with him. She too didn't want a nanny around her newborn.

Fabian walked over to Kylie and kissed her on the cheek. Kylie closed her eyes, relishing the feel of his lips on her skin. She had missed the affection that only Fabian could dish out.

"I'm out. Take care of my baby and make sure you answer your phone," he said looking into her eyes.

"I will."

As Fabian walked out and left, Kylie sat back thinking of what she and Fabian used to be. It seemed as though giving birth to Shai had released all of that built up resentment towards Fabian. The love she had for Fabian had never vanished; if anything, it had become stronger because he had helped her create their lovely daughter. She wanted her child to have both of her parents in the same household, but the memory of Fabian cheating on her haunted Kylie often.

Kylie believed Fabian was sorry for his actions, but could she ever trust him again? She wanted to take a chance on their love once more, but what would the cost be? Could Kylie really get over Fabian giving away what was hers? She thought she couldn't, but whenever she would think of Fabian, a smile would appear on her face. In her mind, no one would compare to the passion they once shared.

Kylie decided she would talk to someone about it before making the decision to get her family back.

Fabian sat on the jet thinking of Kylie. He had no clue as to how he would get her back, but he knew he had to think of something. Everything in his life was beginning to fall into place, but he knew he wouldn't feel complete until Kylie was back in his life. He knew he had a lot of making up to do, but he was willing to go through anything just for her. He felt the confirmation when Kylie birthed their daughter. It was then when he felt an indisputable unity with Kylie.

His thoughts then drifted to Ava and her confession. She was the one who had left him for another woman. Back then, Fabian's ego was bruised because he had lost his first love to another female. At the time, Ava expected Fabian to just accept it and move on. So he did, and that's when he had met Fancy. Now, it was Ava's turn to accept the rejection and move on. Fabian had not an ounce of guilt for being honest with Ava because she had done the same thing to him. He was sure that she was hurt, but the only woman he craved was Kylie, and she was the only person who held the key to his heart.

****

It was a visiting day for Kylie's household. Kellan had come over, along with her Aunt Fallon. Ana and Calise had stopped by with more gifts for the baby. Also Monet had come with Kenyon. Kenyon was so overprotective of his baby sister. He made sure everyone washed their hands before they touched her, which Kylie thought was cute.

Everyone sat in the living room chatting and eating.

"I bet Fabian been calling all day," Kellan asked.

Kylie rolled her eyes. "Girl, he's working my damn nerves. He wants to know everything that's going on with her. Then had the nerve to ask me did I feed her," she chuckled causing everyone break out in laughter.

"That boy is a mess. He was just like that with this one," Monet said pointing to Kenyon.

Kylie asked Monet to follow her to the bedroom. When they walked in, Monet sat on the chaise.

"I wanna talk to you about something," Kylie told her.

"What's wrong?"

"Nothing serious. I just really miss Fabian. It's crazy because I've felt this way for a while, but I'm scared to give him another chance because of what happened. I needed somebody's advice, and since you know him better than I do, I thought I would ask you."

"I know you miss him just by the look in your eyes. I don't blame you for having second thoughts because I would too. I've been in your position before so I know how you feel."

"Really?" Kylie asked.

"Yes, with their father. We had been together for almost eleven years, I gave him five beautiful sons and he turned around and cheated on me with his ex. I forgave him and took him back, but he did it again. So after that last time, I packed up my boys and I left. After about a year, we were divorced, and of course he tried to get me to come back, but I wasn't having that," Monet shot. Kylie laughed at her while continuing to listen.

"But I honestly think that Fabian has learned his lesson. I'm sure he regrets his decision too. He tells me all the time, 'Mama, I messed up.' But if that's the one you wanna be with, then go for it. I think you're having second thoughts because you're scared of what others would think. Am I right?" Monet asked her.

"Yeah, that's part of it," she admitted.

"Girl, you can't worry about what other people have to say. You'll go crazy letting other people's opinions run your life. I know you still love him, and I know for a fact that he loves you. You two have this gorgeous baby here, great careers and Kenyon loves you. I say work it out. But before you do, take your time and make sure this is the right decision. Don't rush into anything, okay?"

"Thank you. You remind me so much of my mom," Kylie said hugging her.

"You're welcome. You'll always be my daughter, no matter what happens between you and Fabian."

CHAPTER 35

Fabian had finally completed his album within the two-week time span. He felt great about his work because he knew he had put all of his heart and soul into it. He still wasn't ready to sign to a major record company. Fabian wanted to build his own company, so he opted to remain independent for the time being. He was on his way back home to see his kids. Lord knew that he had missed Shai and Kenyon dearly. He wasn't used to being away from them this long since he had been on house arrest for the last several months.

Kylie made sure to FaceTime Fabian every night just as he had requested. Kenyon had even stayed with her a couple nights. Today, Kylie was going to surprise Fabian and pick him up from the airport with the kids. She found herself thinking of Fabian more than she had before. Kylie thought about the talk that she had with Monet, and she decided to take it slow with Fabian. She wasn't ready to let him know that she wanted to work on their relationship yet. She figured she would just let it flow.

While softly bumping Alex Isley "About Him", Kylie made her way through the airport. She parked and sat quietly going through her phone. Alex' lyrics moved through her as she sang, *"When I call you darling can't help but smile, time could stop forever and that would be fine."*

"Look, Kylie, there's my dad," Kenyon told her.

Kylie looked up and saw Fabian and his entourage coming off of the jet. Fabian appeared to be happy while talking to one of his cousins. Kylie couldn't help but get moist at the sight of him. He looked very scrumptious in a black bomber jacket with a black tee and some black Gucci jeans. He completed the look with some black high top Gucci sneakers and a snapback cap. Kylie blew her horn, which got everyone's attention. Fabian smiled when he saw her car and made his way over to her. He opened the door smiling from ear to ear.

"What's up, Kylie? What are you doing here?"

"I wanted to pick you up with the kids."

Fabian looked in the back seat and saw Kenyon cheesing along with Shai in her car seat. Immediately, Fabian opened the back door to greet his kids.

"What's up, Kenyon? You missed me?" he said kissing his cheek.

"Yeah, dad. Can we go to Monkey Joes one day?"

"Yeah, we can go."

Fabian looked at Shai, who was wide awake looking as cute as she wanted to be.

"Hey, daddy's baby. Did you miss me too?" Fabian cooed to her, taking her out of her car seat and kissing her.

Shai just stared back at him while he kept cooing in her face. After kissing her for five minutes straight, Fabian finally put her back in her car seat.

"So where are we going?" Fabian asked, sitting in the passenger seat.

"To get something to eat."

"Let me text my security guard so he can meet us."

Kylie drove off, then headed for Famous Dave's. She had been craving some BBQ and knew she would be satisfied with them. When they arrived, they were seated right away. Kenyon sat next Fabian while Shai remained in her car seat. His security guard had met them there and was seated at the table next to them.

"So how was recording? Did you make some hot songs?" Kylie asked.

"Yeah, I was definitely inspired on this album. The first single should be out next week. I can't wait until it comes out."

Kylie smiled. "Me either. I'm supposed to go to Fashion week in NYC soon. I really don't wanna go," she sighed.

"Why not?" he asked biting into some ribs.

"'Cause I don't wanna be away from Shai for a whole week, but then I don't wanna take her either. But this was planned before I got pregnant."

"Who are you leaving her with?" Fabian asked with a raised eyebrow.

"Your mother."

"She'll be fine. I'll be with her for some days. Don't worry; I ain't gon' let shit happen to my baby. Ain't that right, Kenyon?"

Kenyon nodded his head up down, which caused Kylie to laugh. He always knew what to say to ease her mind and Kylie appreciated that. Kylie knew in her heart that she didn't want to be without Fabian, but she was scared to let her guard down.

****

The week had finally come for Kylie to go to New York. She had been dreading this day for a while now. She couldn't stand leaving Shai and wished she could get out of it, but she had an obligation that she had to meet. Kylie kissed the baby for the hundredth time before handing her over to Monet.

"Uggh, I can't stand it," Kylie whined.

"Girl, she'll be alright. Fabian will be back here tomorrow to get her. Now go head before you miss your flight," Monet smirked.

Kylie sighed, not wanting to go. "Okay, don't be alarmed if I call you too much," Kylie warned her.

"I already know the deal. Now bye, girl."

Kylie raced to the airport where she met Kellan and some of her other staff. They boarded the plane and she decided to get some much-needed rest.

When they landed, Kylie got a call from Trace.

"Hello."

"What's up, Ky? Where you at?" he asked

"We just landed in NYC. Why? What's up?"

"I was calling to tell you that I rented a suite for you and Kellan. It's yours if you want it," he offered.

"Aww, that was sweet. Sure we'll take it."

"Aight then. I'll see you in a little while."

Kylie hung up, then immediately called Monet to check on Shai. After making all of her calls, she and Kellan had to go meet with the designer Isabel Marant, who she was styling for. After going over specifics and picking out the pieces, Kylie made her way to the hotel. She felt so weird being without her baby.

During the meeting, Kylie's thoughts were consumed with Shai. She knew that her passion to be a stylist was dwindling away. Her heart wasn't in it like it had been before. She was tired of working for rude and sometimes insulting people. It was time for her to retire.

"Girl, Trace hooked us up. I am loving this suite," Kellan gushed.

"Yeah, it's nice," Kylie responded dryly.

"Eww, what's wrong with you?" Kellan asked noticing her somber mood.

Kylie plopped down on the bed. "I'm ready for this to be over so I can get back home to my baby."

Kellan giggled. "Aww, your mommy instincts are kicking in," she joked.

"Shut up."

All of a sudden, Trace had walked into the room without knocking.

"What's up, ladies?" he asked giving them a hug.

Kylie stepped back from their hug. "How did you get in here?"

"My suite is connected to this one, nosy," he joked.

"Nosy my ass. Don't be running up on us like that. You know we packed the heat," Kellan teased.

"My bad," Trace said with his hands in a surrender pose. "I forgot y'all was thuggin'. Aye, y'all ready to go hit the scene?"

"I don't feel like it," Kylie told him.

Kellan smacked her lips. "Come on, Ky. You haven't been out since you had the baby. Let's have some fun," she tried to persuade her.

"Yeah, come on, girl. Everything's on me," Trace added.

"Let me think about it," Kylie said with a smile.

"I'll put an outfit together for you," Kellan said excitedly.

"Aight, I'll give you girls some time to get cute. And by the way, you're looking good, Kylie, for someone who just had a baby," he smiled lustfully.

"Thanks, Trace," she said rolling her eyes.

****

After having what fun she could have, Kylie got to work. Her days consisted of nothing but fashion and labels. The fashion show had gone great, and Kylie was so relieved. It was her last night in New York and she was more than ready to get back home. Kylie called Monet to check on the baby, but was told that Fabian had her. She dialed Fabian's number, and he answered on the second ring.

"What up, Ky?"

"Nothing. What is Shai doing?"

"She's sitting here fighting her sleep. What's up with you?"

Kylie laid back on the pillow. "Just got back to the hotel not too long ago. I'm ready to see my honey," she smiled.

"I'm ready to see you too," Fabian flirted.

"I see you got jokes. Where y'all at?" she asked changing the subject.

"We're in Vegas right now."

"What?!" Kylie shrieked.

Fabian laughed hard. "I'm just playing. We're at my house."

"Fabian, do not play, especially with my baby," she laughed.

"Nah, but she good, man. Enjoy your last night in New York. Don't call me no more tonight, unless we're talking about me and you."

"Me and you, huh? What do you mean by that?" she asked smiling on the inside.

"You know exactly what it means. Don't act like you new to this shit."

"Well, maybe you'll get a call, maybe you won't," she teased him.

"Aight. I'll be waiting."

"Byeeeee," Kylie sang, then hung up.

Kylie had to admit that she enjoyed Fabian's flirtatious words. She felt even better that Fabian was feeling the same way she was. Kylie packed up everything so she could be ready for her flight in the morning, and Kellan came into the room with her laptop.

"Ky, have you heard Fabian's new song? It is so cute," she gushed.

"No, what is it called?"

"It's called 'Pieces Of My Heart,' and guess who he talks about?"

"Who?"

"You," Kellan said with excitement.

"Yeah right," Kylie replied with disbelief.

"I'm so serious, and plus his kids. Here; listen to it."

Kellan gave her the laptop and Kylie put on the headphones. She pressed played and listened as his voice came through the speakers. It felt good to finally hear some new music from Fabian. Just his voice alone caused Kylie's heart to play hopscotch in her chest. The entire song was about her and the kids. On the last line of the song, he stated, "I never stopped loving you. You will always have a piece of my heart."

Kylie began to tear up after hearing the song. No one had ever made a song for her. Kylie felt so overwhelmed by her emotions. She was tired of fighting her love for Fabian. On that day of his video shoot, she had fallen in love with him. Yes, there was still a burn from his infidelity, but she was more than willing to put it all behind her and start over with Fabian. Her only obstacle would be revealing her forgiveness to Fabian.

"Are you crying?" Kellan asked, sitting next to her.

"No," Kylie smiled through her tears.

"Liar. Why are you crying?"

Kylie took the back of her hands and wiped away her tears. "'Cause I still love Fabian, but I don't know how to tell him."

"Just tell him. Why is that so hard?" Kellan questioned.

Kylie looked at her and smacked her lips. "The same reason you still like Braylon, but refuse to tell him," Kylie shot.

Kellan rolled her eyes. "We're not talking about me. We're talking about you."

"Whatever, Kells. I'm going to take a shower."

"You're gonna have to wait after me!" Kellan shot up and ran in before her.

"You tramp! You know you always run out the hot water!" Kylie yelled.

Kylie gathered her things, then went over to Trace's suite. She knocked three times before he answered the door.

"What's up?" he asked dressed in a wife beater and basketball shorts.

"Can I please use your shower?" Kylie asked sweetly.

"Yeah. Come on."

Kylie walked into his bathroom, then closed the door. She began to undress and took her phone out of her robe to play some music. After selecting her Fabolous playlist, she got in the shower.

Trace sat in the bedroom thinking of ways to make Kylie's his. He had grown tired of just being her friend. He wanted Kylie to be his lady and was willing to do anything to make that happen. He was aware that Kylie was forever linked to Fabian since they had a child together, but Trace was willing to overlook that. Kylie had been teasing him for years, and it was time to take their friendship to the next level.

An idea popped into Trace's head as he sat on the bed. He waited about two minutes before he tiptoed into the bathroom. He could hear Kylie singing with the song that was playing behind the shower door. Trace couldn't resist getting a peek of Kylie's voluptuous ass. He took out his iPhone and turned on the camera. Trace took a peek and saw that Kylie was facing forward, so he hurried and snapped two pictures before she turned around. Since Trace turned his flash off, Kylie had no idea that he was taking pictures of her body. Trace quietly made his exit as Kylie prepared to get out of the shower. She dried herself and threw on a hotel robe. Opening the door, she saw that Trace was seated on his bed smoking a cigar.

"Thanks, fam."

"No problem," he said with a smirk.

CHAPTER 36

Kylie had just landed in Milwaukee and couldn't wait to get to her muffin. Since she had left her car at the airport, she hopped in and made her way over to Fabian's. Kellan had ridden with her so Kylie had to drop her off at home, but she went to Fabian's first.

Once she arrived, she noticed that the family's cars were parked in his driveway.

"Your boo is here," Kylie teased Kellan, referring to Braylon.

"Girl, bye." Kellan said trying to mask her smile.

Kylie walked in and made her way to the kitchen since that was where she'd heard the noise.

"Hello everyone," Kylie greeted them.

She walked over to Fabian who had Shai in his arms. She immediately picked her up. "Oh, I've missed my honey. Hi, Shai. Did you miss, mommy," Kylie said rubbing on her head and kissing her constantly.

"I know you are glad you're back at home," Monet said.

Kylie gave her a knowing look. "Yes. She's just gonna have to travel with me in the future. This was torture," she giggled.

"Now you see how I felt," Fabian told her.

"Oh, here, Monet; I have goodies for you," Kylie said giving her a bag full of purses and clothes from the fashion show.

"Thank you, sweetie. You always think of me."

"What's up, Kellan?" Fabian greeted her as he stood by the counter.

"What's going on with you? I love your new song," Kellan told him.

"Thanks." He then turned to Kylie. "How do you like it?" he asked her.

Kylie smiled. "It's nice. I like it."

Interrupting their staring match was her cell phone. She noticed it was Trace, so she decided to step out into the hallway with the baby still in her arms.

"What's up, Trace?" she answered in her low voice.

"I was seeing if you made it home safely."

"Yeah I'm here. Thanks," she said rushing off of the phone.

"Wait, Kylie, I've been meaning to talk to you about something," he said.

Kylie rolled her eyes because she was just with him, and he never mentioned he had something to talk about. "Like what?"

"Listen; I've been patient, and I'm feeling you like crazy. But I think you knew that already. I'm trying to see if we could work on a relationship."

Kylie looked at the phone in disbelief. *What is this nigga on?* she thought to herself.

"Trace, what are you talking about? I told you I only would like a friendship," she said as nice as she could.

"I'm tired of being just your friend. I think we could be a real-life power couple."

Kylie released a sigh. She couldn't understand why Trace couldn't be content with their friendship. "Listen, Trace; you know I love you like a brother. And I cherish our friendship. I wouldn't want to mess that up," she reasoned.

"Well, I'm willing to settle for something else," he suggested.

"What do you mean *something else*?"

"Maybe a lil' bit of bedroom action."

"What the hell did you just say to me?" Kylie asked appalled by his statement.

"You heard me, Kylie. I'm sure you know what that means."

"Are you out of your fucking mind? Don't ever in your life come at me like that again," she ordered, hanging up the phone.

Kylie couldn't believe Trace had called her asking for sex. It was as if he had transformed into Dr. Jekyll and Mr. Hyde. She was definitely going to block his number from here on out. She truly wanted to know what had gotten into him. Before she'd left New York, everything between them had been good.

Kylie walked back into the kitchen with a pissed off look on her face. Kellan noticed that her facial expression had changed.

"What's wrong with you?" she asked Kylie.

Kylie shook her head as she rubbed on the baby's back. Trace had really killed her mood with his disturbing call.

Minutes later, her phone signaled that she had a text message. She opened the message and couldn't believe her eyes. It was a picture of her naked when she had taken a shower in Trace's room. Under the picture was a message: *Kylie, I've been daydreaming about this pic all day. Can you at least think about what I said?*

Instantly, all of the color drained from her face as she tried to process what she had just seen. *That bastard was taking pictures of me while I was in the shower! I can't believe this fucking pervert!* she screamed inside.

"Kylie, are you okay?" Kellan asked her again knowing that something wasn't right.

Kylie shook her head and frantically began to grab her belongings. "Yeah. Um… we gotta go."

Fabian gave Monet a puzzled look while trying to see what had changed in a matter of five minutes. Fabian knew Kylie like he knew every Tupac song, and he could tell that something was not right with her. She was still packing all of Shai's things while trying to keep her tears from falling.

"Aye, mama, keep an eye on the baby real quick. Kylie, come here," he demanded while leaving out of the kitchen.

Kylie sighed before she handed Monet the baby and then followed him out of the kitchen.

Fabian led Kylie up to his bedroom and he closed the door.

****

Kellan sat at the breakfast bar having a conversation with Monet. She too loved Monet's personality, which made her feel at ease around her. Braylon walked in surprised to see Kellan. He couldn't help but fantasize on how her firm legs would feel wrapped around his waist at that very moment. He often thought about her and wished that they were at least still friends.

"What's up, Kellan?" he greeted her while licking his lips.

"Hi, Braylon," she replied, feeling butterflies in her stomach.

"Y'all need to get a room," Adrian blurted out.

Kellan laughed. "What are you talking about?"

"Come on, y'all. It's obvious that you guys like each other," Monet reasoned.

"Mama, Kellan don't be tryin' to mess with your boy. She said I play too many games," Braylon said with a grin.

Kellan cut her eyes at him. "You do."

"I'll admit I used to, but I'm on something different," Braylon declared as he looked her square in the eyes.

Kellan rolled her eyes, not impressed with his words. She figured if he lied before, then it would be no problem for him to lie again.

"You don't believe me?" he asked.

Kellan shook her head. "I don't believe words. Actions will tell me what I need to know," she smirked.

"Aight, well, how about you let me show you then? We can start over," Braylon suggested.

"I don't know."

Braylon sucked his teeth. "Come on, girl. Stop acting like that. I'm being for real," he told her, looking into her eyes.

Kellan began to smirk. "We'll see, Braylon, but I can't make you any promises."

****

"Aye, what's wrong with you? And don't lie," Fabian demanded.

Kylie contemplated if she should tell Fabian about her dilemma. She knew Fabian had an issue with her and Trace's friendship and didn't want to hear, "I told you so." So Kylie broke out in tears not knowing what to do. Fabian grabbed her and pulled her into her chest. He knew it was something big because Kylie didn't cry over anything.

"Tell me what's bothering you," he said lifting her face.

"It's Trace."

Fabian's face contorted into a mean scowl. "What he do?"

"He sent me a disturbing text."

"About what?"

Kylie began to tell him everything that had transpired. She made sure to tell every detail, including the shower situation.

"Do you see why I told you to stop fuckin' with him? He had a hidden agenda all along. I told you he wanted to fuck you," he seethed.

"Fabian, I thought he was my friend. How the fuck was I supposed to know that he would violate my privacy and take a picture of me in the shower?" she snapped.

"You were supposed to listen to your man! You think I just be tellin' you shit just to hear my voice? I'm a nigga so I know when another man wants my lady!" he barked.

"You know what? Fuck you! You sittin' up here screaming at me like I did something!" Kylie yelled and tried to walk to the door but was stopped by Fabian.

"Hold on. I didn't mean to yell," he reasoned as he pulled her back in front of him.

Kylie continued to look away, still pissed at his words.

"Let me handle it," Fabian told her.

Kylie shook her head feverishly. "No, it's nothing to handle. I'm not even going to respond to his stupid ass," she insisted.

Fabian smacked his lips, not liking what she'd just said. "Man, don't insult me like that. What kind of man would I be if I allowed this to happen? Plus, I know you don't want those pictures to leak on the internet. Just text him and act like you agree with his plan. I'll take care of the rest. I got you," he instructed as he hugged her.

"Thank you," she said gazing into his eyes.

Fabian tenderly kissed her forehead, then the tip of her nose. Kylie closed her eyes and savored the feel of his lips.

"You trust me?" Fabian whispered.

Kylie shrugged. "I don't know. Should I?" she replied becoming lost into his existence.

"I know I fucked up in the past, but I have learned from my mistakes. I know it takes time to get back the trust I once had, but I'm willing to do whatever for you to be in my life. I need you, Kylie. I'm willing to do everything on your terms."

Without saying a word, Kylie found Fabian's lips and began to strike them with hers. As soon as their lips connected, they both felt a familiar electricity run through their bodies. This was the moment that Fabian had been dying for. He needed Kylie just like he needed the arteries in his heart.

Kylie swirled her tongue with his as she unbuckled his belt. Fabian took off her shirt, exposing her push-up bra that made her D cups look even more scrumptious.

While continuing to kiss her, Fabian smashed Kylie up against the wall. Kylie hadn't been sexed in months and just the thought of Fabian penetrating her made her wetter. He pulled off his shirt, showcasing his perfectly crafted pecs with tattoos decorating them. He then slid Kylie's skirt up and her thong off, and he cherished her neatly shaven kitty.

"I'm about to *rock* this pussy," he told her in a husky voice.

Fabian picked her body up as he kissed and licked her neck. Kylie couldn't take the foreplay any longer; she was ready for some extreme fucking.

Fabian's finger found her wetness. "Damn, she wet," Fabian whispered, sliding his finger in and out of her pussy.

"Oooh, Fabian. Right there, baby," Kylie panted.

"You like when daddy play with his wet pussy?" he taunted her as his thumb began to rub her clit in a circular motion.

"Ssss...Yes," she squealed.

Fabian then put another finger inside of her and started to work her wet walls. He could feel her clench his fingers.

"This still my pussy?" he whispered.

"Yes, baby."

Fabian continued to torture her with his fingers. Kylie could feel her muscles contract as her legs began to shake. Soon after, her creamy juices painted Fabian's fingers. Kylie came long and hard.

"Turn around," Fabian demanded.

Kylie did as she was told and leaned over the dresser with her ass in the air. The sight of Kylie's ass caused Fabian's dick to get brick hard. He grabbed his shaft and slid all the way inside of Kylie's juicy pussy. It took everything in Fabian not to scream out like a little bitch. Her tight walls clamped Fabian's manhood as he struggled not to bust his nut.

"Come on, daddy; beat it up," Kylie purred.

Fabian happily obliged and began to pound in and out of her wet gushy walls. He spanked each ass cheek as he attacked Kylie's g-spot. Kylie almost felt crazed from the sexual pleasure that Fabian was presenting to her.

"Oooh, baby, I'm about to cum," she whined clenching the dresser.

Minutes later, Kylie came for the second time. Fabian felt her creamy fluids coat his dick. He gripped her hips and continued to go in deeper. Kylie could almost feel him in her stomach, that's how deep Fabian was.

"This the best pussy ever," Fabian grunted as he felt his dick tingle.

Fabian couldn't hold it any longer. His nut was coming and with a full force.

"Shit," Fabian grunted, then exploded inside of Kylie.

Panting as if they had just run a marathon, they both stumbled over to the bed. Fabian pulled her closer to him where he looked into her eyes. He promised himself that he was going to do right by Kylie this time. Being without her was tormenting, and he knew he couldn't live without her.

"I love you more than anything," he told her.

"I love you too, baby," Kylie smiled.

****

One week later...

Kylie had just sent Trace a confirmation text about meeting up with him. She was so disgusted with him that the sight of his name made her nauseous. Kylie honestly thought he was one of her genuine friends, but he had proven that he didn't have her best interest at heart at all.

Lately, Fabian had been coming around a lot more, trying to keep her mind at ease. He knew that this situation was causing more stress for Kylie. He could see that Kylie was hurt about the break up with her friendship with Trace. Fabian hated for her to be in this position, so that's why he chose to step in and handle it. He wanted Kylie to know that he had her back in any circumstance. To Fabian, Kylie was his everything, and he refused to let anybody disrespect her.

CHAPTER 37

Trace walked inside of the Pfister hotel in downtown Milwaukee with a smile sketched on his face. He had been waiting for this day for a long time now. He would finally have Kylie in the way he had been yearning for. Trace had been longing for Kylie's body since the day he had met her. Yes, he may have approached the situation in an unusual manner, but he wanted her in the worst way. Trace didn't think it would be that easy for Kylie to agree to it, but she did, and he was ecstatic.

Trace checked into his presidential suite and made his way to the elevator. Thoughts of Kylie plagued his mind. She was truly one of a kind, and he couldn't wait to savor her juices. He walked inside and got right to work. Trace popped open a bottle of Champagne and skillfully filled two glasses to the brim. Since he wanted Kylie to look good for him, he purchased a La Perla lingerie set.

After placing rose petals all over the bed and lighting scented candles, Trace went to take a quick shower. Kylie was expected to be there in approximately twenty minutes. He scrubbed his body down, making sure he cleansed every crevice. After applying lotion to his body and spraying on his Marc Jacobs cologne, Trace awaited Kylie's arrival. After waiting for what seemed like forever, Trace heard a knock on the door. He shot up with excitement and ran toward the door. He rubbed his hands together and slowly opened the door.

"Trace... What's going on fam'?" Fabian greeted him, bombarding his way inside of the room. Trace stood with this perplexed look on his face, wondering why Fabian was there.

"Aye, what's up? What you doin' here?" Trace asked closing the door.

Fabian ignored his question as he looked around the suite. "Damn, you poppin' Dom P tonight. What's the special occasion?"

"I guess Kylie told you, huh?" Trace asked, shaking his head as he leaned on the back of the couch.

Fabian glared at him. "You fuckin' right! She told me! Since when did you have to do all of this extra shit for some pussy?" Fabian barked.

Trace sucked his teeth. "I knew her stupid ass was gon' go running back to you."

"Mothafucka, you damn right. And don't let another insult come out of yo' fuckin' mouth again," Fabian threatened.

"Man, fuck what you talkin' about. This shit ain't got nothing to do with you. It's between me and Kylie," Trace seethed.

"Nah, you got the game fucked up. When it has something to do with my woman, then it's between all of us, bitch."

Trace plastered a surprised look on his face. "Oh shit. Y'all back together? I know she didn't go back to you as bad as you dogged her ass! You're the same dude that cheated on her; now y'all a happy couple now? Get the fuck outta here!" he yelled, hating the fact that Kylie was back with Fabian.

"You're a jealous bitch. Why you so mad that she chose me?" Fabian smirked.

Trace waved his hand dismissively. "Man, get over yourself. I'm the one that was there for Kylie when your bitch ass decided to dip off with your ex. Whatever she needed, I had it there before she could finish her sentence. So, yeah, I feel like she chose the wrong nigga. You ain't gon' do shit but cheat on her again," Trace smiled.

Fabian shook his head. "You know what? I was coming here to whoop your ass. But I got something even better."

Trace scoffed. "Nigga, you ain't got shit on me," he countered.

"Oh yeah? Take a look at this," Fabian said as he gave him a picture.

Trace looked at the picture with a smug look on his face. "What the fuck this supposed to mean?"

"Oh, so you don't know who that is in the picture?" Fabian asked incredulously.

"Nah man," he replied looking away.

"Come on, Trace. Your memory can't be that bad. You're telling me you don't remember Shontelle aka Xavier? I believe you two used to be an item before you discovered she really had a dick," Fabian said laughing.

Trace threw the picture across the room. "Man, you don't know what the fuck you're talking about!" he yelled, becoming infuriated by the minute.

"Damn, did I strike a nerve? It's funny how you don't know her, I mean him, because I actually had a conversation with him. Nigga, I got connections, and when word get out that I was looking for some dirt on you, my fucking phone wouldn't stop ringing. He told me y'all were together for a while before you discovered he had something extra hanging between his legs. Oh yeah; you also paid him off so he wouldn't tell your little secret," Fabian smiled knowing he had Trace right where he wanted him.

"Man, fuck you. Nobody will believe that shit."

Fabian gave him a twisted look. "Are serious? Here's the proof right here. I told you, don't fuck with me, but you wanted to learn the hard way. Now erase those fuckin' pictures on your phone or your little secret will be revealed to the world," Fabian snapped, while walking out. He stopped right by Trace's ear before leaving. "Guess what? That pussy got my name all over it. You'll never taste it, fam."

Fabian walked out of the room without uttering another word. Trace looked at the picture on the ground and picked it up. He thought that he had done a great job at hiding his past. He knew that this could potentially damage his reputation along with his career. He was so angry at that fact that Fabian had seen him in a vulnerable state. Fabian had backed him into a corner with nowhere to run. So he did the only thing that was logical at that point and erased anything that had to do with Kylie out of his phone and also his mind.

****

Fabian walked into Kylie's home feeling proud. He'd promised Kylie that he would take care of everything and he had accomplished that. He made his way to the bedroom where he found Kylie sitting in her bed feeding Shai. They both looked at one another without saying a word. Fabian took off his shoes and jacket, then lay across the bed staring at the ceiling. Kylie was waiting for him to tell her about his encounter with Trace. From the looks of things, it seemed like things didn't go as planned. Fabian looked over at Kylie thanking God that he had the family he had always wanted. Kylie didn't know it, but

Fabian was willing to fight tooth and nail for her to be an everlasting fixture in his life.

"Is this a 'don't ask, don't tell' moment?" Kylie asked.

"Yeah. Just know everything is cool. Aight?" He looked at her with a reassuring look.

"Okay. I'll take your word for it," she smiled.

"You trust me?" Fabian asked with his eyes closed.

"Yes."

"Do you love me?"

Her smile widened even brighter. "Always, daddy."

EPILOGUE

Three years later...

Fabian sat on the set of his first movie. He'd never thought about acting, but when Will Packer reached out to him about the perfect role for him, Fabian accepted. After months of taking acting classes, he felt he was ready to be on the big screen.

While taking a short break, Fabian reflected on the last three years of his life. God had truly blessed him with a great family and great career. His last two albums were certified platinum, and he had even started his own label.

Interrupting his thoughts was his phone signaling that Kylie was trying to FaceTime him. He answered and Kylie's face appeared.

"Hi, honey. What are you doing?" she asked with a towel wrapped around her head.

"Sitting in the trailer. What's up with you?"

"Nothing. I miss you and so does the kids. We just wanted to say hi... Wait a minute. Here's Kenyon." Kylie passed the phone to Kenyon and he began talking.

"Hey, dad. My report card came yesterday, and I got A's and B's. My football game is on Saturday. You think you'll be able to come?" Kenyon asked.

"Yeah, I'm coming home Friday. You know I wouldn't miss your game," Fabian smiled.

"That's what's up. Wait... Shai, I'm talking right now!" Kenyon scolded Shai who was trying to grab the phone. "Yeah, dad... but I'm supposed to play the quarterback position on Saturday. Here go, Shai." Kenyon passed the phone to Shai.

"Hi, daddy. When are you coming home? I haven't seen you in like five years," Shai exaggerated, which caused Fabian to laugh.

"Daddy comin' home Friday. You been a good girl for your mama?" he asked.

"Yeah, but, daddy, Kenyon was being mean to me last night. He told me I was adopted, and he made me cry," she spoke with a sad face.

"You're not adopted, and I'ma beat Kenyon's ass for telling you that too," he promised.

"Oh, can I have a cell phone?"

Seconds later, you can hear Kylie in the background telling her to hurry up.

"We'll talk about it when I come home," he told her, knowing he wasn't getting a three-year-old a phone.

"Okay, I love you, daddy." Shai passed the phone back to Kylie.

"They have been going at it all day. You don't even know what I've been going through today," she giggled.

"They been stressing my baby, huh?"

"Hell yeah. When are you gonna make time for your wife?" she asked

"Soon. I promise when this movie is done, I'm taking you on a vacation. Just me and you."

Kylie smiled. "I can't wait. Me and the kids are about to meet up with Kellan so she can pick up her dress."

"Word? The wedding is next month, right?"

"Yes, sir. She's about to be a Bryant. I can't believe it," Kylie chuckled.

"Yeah, that's crazy. Well, I gotta get back to work, so I'll call you later. Oh, and tell Kenyon if he tell my baby she's adopted again, I'ma fuck him up." Fabian chuckled

"Will do. Bye love."

"Aight."

****

Kylie hung up thinking how blessed she was. She was no longer a stylist anymore. Kylie dedicated her time to her jewelry line, which was doing exceptionally well, and her family. Kellan was elected to take Kylie's place, so she was now in charge of the styling business. Kylie never did hear from Trace again. Last she heard, he was starring in his own reality show. A part of Kylie wanted to hate him, but she couldn't bring herself to do it.

After starting over and getting back to that place of happiness, Kylie and Fabian finally got married. She no longer had to search for the love she had always wanted because it was right in her face. Fabian completed her in every way imaginable and she couldn't imagine life without him.

As she thought of Fabian and looked at her daughter and stepson, she smiled. *This is the life. Thank you Lord.*

The End

To receive email notifications of new releases from Charae Lewis, text the keyword "JWP" to 22828!

The Rapper's Delight book discussion will be in the Jessica Watkins Presents reading group on March 8th at 7pm CST. Click HERE to join!

Follow Charae Online:
Facebook: Charae Lewis
Instagram: Charae_Rozay
Twitter: Charae_Lewis
Facebook Group:
https://www.facebook.com/groups/1716797471875878/

The End